Christine Merrill lives o
USA, with her husband, t
pets—all of whom would
computer so they can check their email. She has worked by turns in theatre costuming and as a librarian. Writing historical romance combines her love of good stories and fancy dress with her ability to stare out of the window and make stuff up.

Also by Christine Merrill

A Scandalous Match for the Marquess
'A Mistletoe Kiss for the Governess'
in *Regency Christmas Weddings*

Society's Most Scandalous collection

How to Survive a Scandal

Secrets of the Duke's Family miniseries

Lady Margaret's Mysterious Gentleman
Lady Olivia's Forbidden Protector
Lady Rachel's Dangerous Duke

The Irresistible Dukes miniseries

Awakening His Shy Duchess
A Duke for the Penniless Widow

Wicked Dukes miniseries

To Wed a Devilish Duke

Discover more at millsandboon.co.uk.

TO REDEEM A RAKISH DUKE

Christine Merrill

MILLS & BOON

First published in Great Britain 2025
by Mills & Boon, an imprint of HarperCollins*Publishers* Ltd,
1 London Bridge Street, London, SE1 9GF

www.harpercollins.co.uk

HarperCollins*Publishers*, Macken House, 39/40 Mayor Street Upper,
Dublin 1, D01 C9W8, Ireland

ISBN: 978-0-263-34545-2

12/25

This book contains FSC™ certified paper
and other controlled sources to ensure responsible forest management.

For more information visit www.harpercollins.co.uk/green.

Printed and Bound in the UK using 100% Renewable Electricity
at CPI Group (UK) Ltd, Croydon, CR0 4YY

To Jim, taking another one for the team.

Chapter One

'I have done something terribly foolish.'

Cassandra Fisk stared at the man on the other side of the card table, waiting for further explanation. Her half-brother, Julian, frequently did things that she considered foolish. He was a rake and his pleasures were often unhealthy or unwise.

Julian was also the Duke of Septon. Since he was a peer, there was not much that would not be forgiven by Society. But there was something about the look on his face as he reached for the brandy bottle that said that this time he was having trouble forgiving himself.

She smiled at him as if she hadn't noticed the change in his manner and kept her tone light. 'Foolish? You? Never, darling. I refuse to believe it.'

Julian sighed. And suddenly he looked like someone who'd had a long and unhappy life, even though he was but four years older than she. 'I suppose I should tell you everything. It will be in the papers tomorrow, and all of London will be talking about it. There was a duel.' He took another drink, staring down into the glass as though afraid to meet her gaze.

'Dueling is illegal,' she said, automatically.

'At the time, that fact did not concern me,' he said with a wry smile. 'Quite a bit of liquor had been consumed.'

'And your opponent?' she said, struggling to maintain her smile.

'Westbridge,' he said, refilling his glass.

She had not expected this. 'I thought you were friends.'

'We were,' he replied. 'But he said something inappropriate about Miss Braddock. I could not let it pass.'

'I see.' Julian had been friends with the girl's father, before he'd died, and been tasked with protecting Portia Braddock's honour until she married. If sometimes Cassandra suspected that his feelings for his charge might run deeper than mere duty? She did not dare say.

'You won, of course,' she said cautiously.

'I am here, aren't I?' he replied. 'Whole and undamaged.' He grimaced and drained his glass.

She watched as he reached for the bottle again. 'What of Westbridge?'

'He is… Alive.' But there was something in the pause that said he might not be for long. 'If things do not go well for him, I might not be able to visit you for a while. I might have to leave London.'

Now she had to fight to hide her fear. Westbridge was a duke, just as Julian was. To duel was bad enough. But to kill another peer while doing so would never be forgiven. He would be tried as a murderer in the House of Lords and might be stripped of his title and hung with a silk rope, dying in disgrace that could never be expunged.

'My only regret is that it might cause trouble for you,' he said with a shake of his head. 'The world does not know of your relationship to me. Our father told no one that he had an illegitimate daughter, and now that I've found you, I've been waiting for the best time to announce your addition to the family. But if I have damaged the family name beyond repair…' He poured and drank. 'Perhaps it would be better for your reputation if you had never met me.'

'Nonsense,' she said, reaching out to touch his hand. 'I have always wanted a brother, and I could not have been happier when you sought me out after coming into the title. It was kind to bring me to London and I treasure every moment we've spent together. If my presence is inconvenient for you, I can return to the country where I was raised. But I will not abandon you when you need me, just because of a little scandal.'

'I will arrange a settlement for you, in any case,' he said with a wave of his hand. 'Your company is a blessing, not a burden. It is just that I had hoped to bring you out properly. I wanted the *ton* to see what a delightful girl you are. If only there were more time…' He stared into his glass again as if the dark future rested at the bottom, then splashed some more brandy into it and drank.

Cassandra forced a laugh. 'You speak as if all hope is lost. Westbridge might survive. Someone else might do something that makes your duel pale in comparison.'

'Of course,' he said, giving her an equally forced smile. 'I am sure it will all be forgotten in a day or two. In any case, I should not let it spoil our time together.' He reached for the cards. 'My deal, I think.'

'Of course,' she agreed.

They played piquet for most of the evening, just as they did each Wednesday, when he came to the little house he had bought for her in St John's Wood. She suspected that he used these visits to escape the stress of his week and he needed that release tonight, more than ever. So, she turned their conversation from his troubles, amusing him with stories of her life in the country and the mundane pleasures of her week. It seemed to have worked. When it grew late and he rose to leave, he gave her a genuine smile as he kissed her cheek. 'Thank you for a pleasant evening. I hope I did not worry you earlier. It will probably come to nothing.'

'I'm sure you are right,' she said and followed him out of the house. She watched to see he got safely into his coach, waving after it until she was sure it was well out of sight. Then, she went inside and closed the front door leaning against it, letting her panic bubble to the surface leaving her almost too weak to stand.

She loved him dearly, but she had no illusions about her brother's character. Though he had never been anything but sweet to her, Julian courted scandal the way other men courted the virgins at Almack's. It was the reason he had kept her hidden here, and not announced to the *ton* that he had a long-lost sister. He had wanted the proper time and the perfect way to introduce her to Society so that his sordid reputation would not spoil her chances of making a good match. Though his behaviour was often self-destructive, he always took care not to hurt others with it.

Until today, at least.

He had never done anything as foolish as dueling. Nor would she have imagined that he could wound a friend, much less bring one to the point of death.

She closed her eyes tight and offered a silent prayer that it would not be so. She did not want to see her dear brother a murderer. Could he really be forced to flee the country to avoid prosecution? When he'd suggested that, he'd been worrying for her future and not his own. A tear slid down her cheek as she remembered. It was just like him to think of her before worrying about the risk to himself. Why did he not understand that she would gladly trade this house and everything in it if she could be sure he was safe? She had a home in the country with the people who had raised and loved her as their own child. The Reverend and Mrs Fisk would take her back in a heartbeat, if needed.

Julian had no one but her.

She opened her eyes again, her mind racing. Though it would shock her adoptive father to hear her say it, prayers were useless at a time like this. Action was required. Years of nursing the sick of the parish had left her more than qualified to be of help. She would see to it that Westbridge survived. Perhaps she could even influence him to forgive his enemy, and this whole situation might amount to nothing.

She summoned the housekeeper and asked her to send for the carriage and prepare a selection of medicinal herbs from the still room.

Then, she went upstairs and rang for her maid, changing out of the fine dinner gown Julian had bought for her, and into one of the simple dresses she had worn in the country, a brown cotton with a starched white chemisette filling the neckline. She pulled the pins from her hair and brushed out the curls, pulling them back into a practical style that kept them out of her face and which could be maintained without the help of a servant.

As she reached for an untrimmed bonnet she glanced into the dressing table mirror at the modest and sensible girl reflected there. She smiled, relieved. Since bringing her to town, Julian had spoiled her, sparing no expense to give her the life he felt she deserved. But beneath the satins and lace, she was still a vicar's daughter, and happy to be so.

If London had taught her nothing, she had learned the value of her parents' teachings. The wages of sin were death. Julian's foolish duel was proof of that. If she could manage to keep his friend alive, perhaps the sin could be forgiven and forgotten. With one last glance in the mirror, she tied on her bonnet and went downstairs. Then she collected her little bag of medicines and went out into the night.

* * *

When the carriage arrived at the house of the Duke of Westbridge, she went to the door with a crisp step and knocked. She must act as if it was perfectly natural for an unaccompanied young woman to arrive at the house of a man who was not only unmarried but just as scandalous as her brother. Under the circumstances, allowances should be made when enforcing the rules of etiquette.

The butler opened the door and looked out at her with suspicion.

'I have come to help the surgeon,' she said, giving the servant a no-nonsense smile.

'He has gone home to bed,' the butler replied, unmoving. 'He said there was nothing more that could be done.'

'I am aware of that,' she replied. 'I have been summoned to sit with the patient. He should not be alone.'

The butler considered her story for a moment, then stepped out of the way and allowed her to enter. Without another word, he led her to the stairs and up them to the master bedroom, where the duke was sleeping.

Inside, a single candle guttered on the bedside table and a worried maid sat in a darkened corner, a terrified expression on her face.

Cassandra gave her the same efficient smile she'd offered to the butler. 'It is all right. I am here. You can go now.'

The girl looked from her to the butler in the doorway. 'The doctor told me to wait. To summon him if there was any change.'

'And now I shall be the one to do so,' Cassandra said with a firm nod. She went to the bedside and looked down at the injured man, doing her best to hide her worry. She laid a hand on his forehead, gauging his temperature, and felt the beginnings of a fever. It was good that she had come. He might not have survived the night with only a maid to tend him.

She glanced back at the butler. 'Could you have someone bring a full kettle and a cup? I have feverfew and willow bark in my bag and will get him to take a little, if he wakes.'

'Very good,' the butler said and gave a sharp nod in the direction of the maid who hurried off to get the water, relieved to have something constructive to do.

'You needn't worry,' she said. 'I will watch over him and do everything I can.'

'Thank you.' His anxious tone surprised her. It was not often that she heard such a servant reveal anything like real emotion, especially not with a stranger in the room. For a moment, he looked down on the man in the bed with an almost fatherly affection. Then, he withdrew, leaving her alone with her patient.

She turned back to Westbridge, allowing herself a more thorough examination. Loss of blood had left him worryingly pale and as still as a statue, his skin alabaster, his lips almost blue.

But the injury had done nothing to spoil his looks. He had the sort of classical profile that a sculptor would have loved. His blond hair had not been combed. It swept back from his face in waves, revealing a noble brow. His cheekbones were high and his chin strong, sharp accents framing a sensual mouth.

There was something about those lips that gave her pause. A sense that they'd known pleasure and given it, as well. Though they were tight with pain, the creases at their corners said he smiled often. She imagined the expression: knowing, ironic, perhaps just a bit uneven to take the sting from the wickedness of it. He would have the sort of smile that could make a woman do things she might never risk for another, less beautiful man.

She shook her head and looked away for a moment, gathering her thoughts. She had come here to tend his injury, not to daydream in the nighttime. She had best get down to the business of nursing him.

She pulled back the covers, looking at the bandage that covered the wound on his shoulder. It could use changing, but it appeared that the bleeding had stopped. Why was he so pale?

Then, she stared down at the marks on his arm. It appeared the surgeon had been bleeding him, which was the last thing he needed after such a serious injury. He must have been trying to keep the fever away, but Cassie had her doubts that it would do any good. Infection came from the dirt in the wound, and removing the blood from his arm would not help at all.

She sighed and replaced the sheet, looking at his face again. Though he was sinfully handsome, sleep revealed an innocence that tempted her to touch him. She wanted to smooth the furrows in his brow to hide the evidence of the pain he was in. There had to be a way to ease his suffering.

As if he sensed her presence, his eyes opened and he stared up at her, confused.

They were very blue.

'It's all right,' she said softly, as she surrendered to the desire and laid her hand on his stubbled cheek. 'You are home. I will take care of you. Now, rest.'

He turned his face into her hand, nuzzling against

it for a moment, a wounded animal seeking comfort. Then, he closed his eyes and settled back into an uneasy sleep.

He had expected there to be flames.

There was torment, of a sort. His shoulder throbbed with a pain greater than he'd ever experienced. But he was chilled rather than burning and floating in a darkness so profound that he feared there was no end to it. Perhaps this was the true nature of hell: cold and isolation for all eternity.

Sebastian Morehead had known that he was damned, even before he'd provoked the duel. One could not lead a life of debauchery and not pay for it in the end. He had clinched the matter by picking a fight with Septon. Julian was a devil with a saber and Sebastian a middling swordsman, at best. The duel had been close to suicide, an unforgivable sin that should have ensured damnation.

He had been cowardly, as well. A brave man would have shot himself and not left it to a friend to murder him in the name of honour. That was one more thing added to his crowded ledger when he met St Peter. He would plead guilty on all counts.

But there had been no judgement. At least, none that he could recall. His mind was cloudy, but intact. He remembered the duel, and the thrust that had finished it. There had been a moment of surprise where he'd seen the blade stuck in his shoulder, but felt nothing. Then a searing pain as he'd dropped his weapon and the sight of his own blood dripping on the ground as they'd carried him to the carriage.

And then…

Distant voices. Shrieks of maids. Muttering. Fussing. Liquid being forced between his lips and down his throat. Then, nothing but more pain. Pain and darkness.

He was alive, but not for long. There had been too much blood on the ground. And he was so very cold.

In the distance, he felt a change. It was far away, as if he was at the bottom of a well. The world he remembered was a distant whisper above him. The pounding anguish of his wound as heavy as water between him and reality.

His eyelids were heavy, too. Like lead. That was why it was so dark. It would be so easy to stay asleep, sinking deeper and deeper until there was no going back. But there was something…

He forced his eyes open and looked up into the face of an angel. Dark hair, luminous skin and grey eyes that stared into his with such tenderness he wanted to weep with joy.

'It's all right,' she said. 'You are home. I will take care of you. Now, rest.' She was caressing his face and for a moment, the gentleness of her touch overshadowed the pain in his body and he dared to hope that there might be salvation. This was heaven and undeserving though he was, she said he was home.

He closed his eyes again and returned to the dark.

Chapter Two

That night, Cassandra dozed in a chair next to the bed, waking occasionally to feel the duke's forehead and check his bandages. It was too soon to tell if he would survive. She did not think an infection would take hold until tomorrow. But the injury must be causing him pain for he tossed in his sleep moaning each time he tried to move his arm.

There was no note as to how much laudanum he'd had, and she wondered if she dared risk giving him a little more. It had been hours since the doctor had gone. A few drops would not hurt.

And if he died?

He might do so anyway. The least shc could do was give him an easy passing. She measured out a dose and forced it into him, offering a silent prayer that the Lord would guide her hand.

In the morning, the doctor arrived to visit and stared at her in surprise as she stepped away from the bed. 'What happened to the girl that was here when I left?'

This was the moment she had been fearing. A wrong word might be her undoing. She gave the surgeon a deferent smile. 'She was nothing more than a maid. The family thought it would be better to have someone with nursing experience…' She dropped a curtsy to indicate that she was the one chosen.

The doctor nodded in approval. 'Very good. And what can you tell me of the night?'

She gave him her report and watched as he examined the duke and called for his valet to change the dressings. Then, he looked back to her and suggested she rest while he finished the examination. He rang for the butler, who escorted her to a dressing room adjoining the duke's bedroom, where a cot and washbasin had been set for her, and a breakfast tray left. She smiled in gratitude and refreshed herself, then lay down on the bed to nap.

It was late afternoon when she came out into the bedroom again to find the doctor getting ready to leave. 'I have left medicines,' he said. 'But short of another bleeding to take down the fever, there is little more I can do. If there is family that might wish to visit, I would recommend they come immediately.'

'I will tell them,' she said, doing her best to keep

her face impassive to hide the panic she was feeling. If the newspapers were correct, the Duke had no kin to call for. Just last month, she had seen the obituary of his grandmother. It had said that Westbridge was the last of his line.

She glanced at the bed with a sadness she had not felt before. At a time like this, there should be someone here who knew and loved him. Someone to pray for his soul, rejoice in his recovery, or mourn his passing. He was still young and had probably assumed there was plenty of time to find a wife and beget an heir. If he died now, he would do it alone. It was not fair.

There was only one thing for it. She must see that he did not die. Hadn't she come here to prevent just such a thing? She must remember that the end of this man would be the end of Julian, as well. Both their futures depended on her skill as a nurse.

He could not die.

She gave the doctor an efficient smile and looked over the medicines he had left, most of which would be useless in the face of sepsis. Then, she pulled a chair to the Duke's bedside and settled into it. 'I will be here for him, if he needs anything.'

'See that you are,' the doctor said, and hurried away as if he did not wish to be present when the inevitable happened.

She sneered after him, then looked back to the Duke, laying her hand on his forehead, which was worryingly hot.

He tossed as if trying to avoid her touch, and muttered, 'Too late.'

She took his limp hand, folding the fingers around her own, urging him to respond. 'No, Your Grace. There is still some life in you.'

'Too late,' he repeated. 'I promised. But I thought there was time.'

That was the way of death, she supposed. When it came, it was always too soon. 'You can have all the time in the world,' she coaxed. 'But you have to want it. What happens next is up to you, Your Grace.'

That sounded too formal for the things she needed to tell him. What had Julian called him? 'Sebastian,' she whispered.

He turned his head towards her, leaning towards the word.

She smiled, encouraged. 'You have to fight, Sebastian.'

'To what purpose?' he moaned, but she felt the grip on her hand tighten. 'No one cares.'

'I care,' she said, squeezing back. 'I am here for you, and I am not going anywhere. You are the one who must not leave.' Without thinking, she leaned forward and pressed a kiss onto his forehead. 'Stay with me, Sebastian.'

'For you,' he said. And for a moment, a ghost of a smile, flitted across his lips. 'I would fight dragons.'

She stifled a smile of her own. Apparently, he was not so far gone that he would not try to charm a lady. It was an encouraging sign. 'That will not be necessary,' she whispered, her lips brushing his ear. 'Not until you are better, at least. We will discuss it when you are better. But you must get better. Promise me you will fight.'

He groaned, in response, but she felt a tiny nod.

She let out a sigh of relief. Then, she soaked a rag in cool water, wiped his temples and dampened his lips. 'Be strong, Sebastian. Be strong for me.'

He gave another faint nod before letting out a sigh and settling back into the pillows as if the brief conversation had exhausted him.

She set the cloth aside and sat down again. As the doctor had said, there was little more they could do than wait.

He had been wrong. He was in hell, after all.

One minute, he could swear that his flesh was being scorched from his body. The next, it felt as if he was drowning in an icy lake. There was not a moment between the two extremes when he was himself and free of pain.

But through it all, he heard her voice.

At first, he'd thought it was his grandmother. That was likely nothing more than a fantasy rising out of his guilt and grief. She had been the only one to care if he lived or died.

But that could not be. Grandmama was dead, and this voice was calling him to live. Then he remembered the face of a woman bending over him. Brown hair, grey eyes and skin that glowed like opal in candlelight.

His angel.

She had promised to stay and was beside him through it all. She'd kept assuring him that there would be an end to the misery, if only he would fight. In his sleep, he smiled, thinking of her. He had lost all hope. Then, she had come and brought it back to him. He would not fail her. He could not.

She was at his side, now, pressing a cup to his lips. Something that tasted foul. He turned his head but she insisted. 'I know it is horrid,' she murmured and slipped an arm around his shoulders, cradling him against her body so he could sip. 'But it will help with the fever.'

He didn't need medicine. He just needed to be held like this, so close to her that he could hear her heart beating against his ear. If he could just get his strength back, he would tell her so.

She nudged his mouth with the cup again and he took a sip for her. Then another. He could not remember finishing it, but she must have been satisfied for she took it away and said, 'Now you must sleep.'

He was too tired to argue, so he did.

When at last he woke, it felt as if he had gone for ages without food or water. 'How long?' His throat was dry and the words came out in a hoarse croak.

'Four days since the duel. Two since the fever began.'

He tried to open his eyes to search for her, but they felt as if they were full of sand. When he reached to wipe them clear, a bolt of pain shot through his left shoulder and he dropped his hand to his side again.

'Let me,' she said, cleaning his face with a damp cloth. When his blurry vision cleared, she was just as he remembered, lovely, smiling and holding a pap boat to his lips.

Remembering the medicine he tried to pull away.

'Just water this time,' she said.

He drank eagerly, not stopping until the cup was empty, and watched as she set it aside. He cleared his throat, then said, 'Who?'

'Your nurse.' She reached for a pitcher and poured another drink.

Did she smile thus for all her patients? He hoped not. He wanted to believe that the light in her eyes was all for him. 'Your name?'

'Cassie, Your Grace.' She offered a respectful bow of her head, but her hand remained steady on the boat and he drank again. When she took it away, she asked, 'Do you think you might be able to take nourishment?'

'Please,' he said. What she offered was hardly food at all. Beef tea with oats in it would not keep a man alive. But she followed it with oranges, which were refreshing, and a good red wine which she said would build up the blood. And she fed each mouthful to him, as if he was an infant.

It was embarrassing. He did not like any woman to see him in this state, as weak as the bouillon in the cup. Especially not a woman as lovely as this one. 'Madam, I can manage for myself,' he said, trying to sit up and show her.

'As you wish, Your Grace.' She put a spoon in his uninjured hand and it shook, clattering against the cup and slipping from his fingers.

She nodded as if to say she'd told him so, took away the spoon and offered him the cup. 'You will be yourself again, soon,' she assured him. 'You are through the worst of it. The wound is draining and has begun to heal.' She pressed her hand to his forehead. 'The fever has broken.' Her fingers pressed against his throat. 'Your pulse is stronger than it was yesterday. We must be cautious, of course. You are still weak. But I am pleased with your progress. Tomorrow, or the next day, perhaps, you will have no need of me.'

'No.' He hadn't meant to say it aloud. But she should not be talking of leaving when they'd barely met.

The corners of her mouth twitched, threatening to turn her polite smile into something warmer and more real. 'That is the goal, Your Grace. To grow strong enough to hold your own spoon and wipe your own bottom.'

He laughed; a sound that was almost as weak as his voice had been.

She listened to it and nodded. 'Your lungs are clear. That is good news. Now you must rest. I will wake you in an hour or two and perhaps you can have a bit of egg with your gruel.'

'I can hardly wait,' he said, trying to keep his tone as light as hers was. He did not want to rest. He wanted to keep her talking, just to hear the sound of her voice. 'Read to me, Cassie, and ease me into sleep.'

'Of course, Your Grace.' She picked up the Bible that sat on the table next to her and began to read.

It was quite appropriate, he supposed, for a ministering angel to read from a holy book. But now that he had gotten a good look at her, he was not in the mood for salvation. She had large, clear eyes, and rich mahogany hair that was pulled back from her face in a plain bun. Not a single curl escaped from it.

Her dress was equally plain, brown cotton without so much as a pearl button to lessen the severity. It made no attempt to flatter, but could not disguise her high, full breasts and trim waist. The hands at the end of the long sleeves were soft and gentle. He had felt the touch of them often enough in the last few days and cherished the memories.

When he was well, in a day or maybe two, he would not let her get away. He would have her unpinned and unraveled before she knew what was happening. Then they would discuss a more permanent position in his household. Something that did not involve sick beds and pap boats. He would be the one stroking her temples and feeding her on peeled grapes and champagne ice.

It would be paradise.

But his fantasy faded a little as he paused to listen to her words which were full of love more spiritual than physical. He needed to do something to put her mind on more earthly pursuits. When she finished the psalm she was reading and turned the page to start another, he held up his good hand to stop her. 'You have a lovely voice, my dear. But perhaps we could enjoy something a little less…' He grimaced.

'Holy?' she said with a smile.

'Formal,' he replied.

She set her Bible aside. 'Very well. What would you prefer?'

'There is a book in the drawer of the bedside table that I have already started. My page is marked.'

'If that is what you wish, I am happy to oblige.' She turned to the table beside her, opened the drawer and took out the volume, turning to the marked page. Her eyes scanned down the text.

'He is now in bed with me the first time, and in broad day; but when thrusting up his own shirt and my shift, he laid his naked glowing body to mine...'

The book snapped shut and she stared at him, shocked. 'I cannot read this. It is…'

'Just getting to the good part,' he finished for her. 'Why don't you come sit on the edge of the bed so we might read it together.'

The look she gave him was not one of virginal shock. But neither was she stifling the knowing giggle of a woman who might be amenable to his offer.

Instead, she looked thoughtful, as if weighing and balancing something.

Probably the worth of his soul against the effort she'd taken to save his body. 'You are as horrible as they say,' she said.

He answered with a resigned nod. 'It would be a lie to deny the fact.'

'But I am not,' she said firmly, as if she'd guessed the contents of his mind.

'Are you a nun, perhaps? A sister who views her nursing as a vocation and will not allow earthly things to sully it?'

For a moment, her lips quirked in a moue of distaste, a puckered expression that only made them seem more kissable. Then, she said, 'It is not necessary to take a vow to eschew pornography. One simply needs to be a lady.'

'A lady,' he repeated and smiled. 'Many women are deemed such by merit of their birth. But I have found, when the lights are out, that some of them are women first and ladies second.'

'I am a lady in word and deed,' she added, with a direct stare meant to dash his hopes.

'You have been alone with me in my bedroom for several days,' he said, speculating. 'And your virtue is still intact.'

'Because you have been ill,' she reminded him. 'I would not be here, else.'

'All the same, it is a record of some sort. For both of us,' he added. 'I have never been so long in proximity with such a lovely woman without at least making a suggestion.'

She waved the book he had requested. 'We will have to start your clock again. This was more than a little suggestive. And the answer is no.'

'It is just as well,' he said, giving her a winning smile. 'I am in no condition to treat you as you deserve. But in a day or two, when I am better…'

'I will leave without anything of note taking place,' she said, giving him a dark look.

'We will see about that,' he said, settling back into the pillows and closing his eyes.

Chapter Three

Sebastian was becoming a problem.

Or perhaps she was the problem. She should be thinking of him as His Grace, the Duke of Westbridge, and not as if she had the right to use his Christian name. But there was something about caring for a person as they faced death that created an intimacy that was difficult to put off once the crisis was over. She felt she *knew* him.

Judging by his behaviour, he felt a similar bond with her. He had apologized for tricking her into opening the book in his night table. But there was something in the way he looked at her, the smile full of mischief and the twinkle in his eyes, that made her think his contrition would not last very long.

For example, she was sure he was quite capable of managing his meals, save for some difficulty cutting his meat. But he was still allowing her to feed him, staring at her with puppy-like devotion and taking bites meekly from the fork she offered.

Worse yet, she was allowing him to get away with it and enjoying the looks he gave her. He made her feel special, more friend than nurse. But there was an innate sensuality in the way his mouth closed over the spoon, then opened so his tongue could lick the bowl. It hinted at something she'd never experienced before that was deeper than friendship.

At the end of the day, when she retired to the cot in the dressing room, she did so with an unfamiliar regret. It had come to feel so natural being with him that it was hard to go even this short distance away.

The bed he lay in was wide. There was ample room for two. The pillows were soft, the sheets cool and white. She could lie by his side, close but separate. And if, by accident or intent, their bodies touched…

'Cassie?'

She blinked in surprise as the fantasy dissolved. He was staring at her, probably hungry. The maid had just brought up his tray and she was woolgathering as the food grew cold. She smiled in apology and began slicing the beef into small bites and peeling and sectioning the orange.

And why was she doing it? The cook could do as much in the kitchen, if she asked. His valet could change the bandage if it was needed. The house was filled with servants to attend to any need. It was time for her to admit that the danger had passed and he no longer needed her nursing. Perhaps, after luncheon, she would pack her bag and take her leave.

But not just yet. She tucked a napkin beneath his chin and put a pillow behind his head so he might sit up.

He opened his mouth, dutifully and waited.

She popped a slice of orange into it.

He chewed and swallowed, watching her. Then, he licked his lips.

Her breath caught in her throat. It was as if she could feel teeth and tongue against her skin, tasting her. She swallowed as well, trying to chase the feeling away. 'You are strong enough to feed yourself today, I think.'

'Do you?' he said and held out his good hand for the fork.

He was staring at her again and she was unable to look away. When she tried to pass him the utensil it dropped uselessly into the bedclothes.

He grabbed her hand, his fingers gently twining with hers. Then, slowly, he pulled it forward until his lips touched the pulse point on her wrist. His tongue darted out again, tracing designs on her skin, and he nipped her, just as she'd imagined.

She was holding her breath again. She let it out in a slow sigh but made no effort to pull away. Her heart was racing. He must be able to feel the pulse against his lips. The knowledge made it beat even faster.

Now he was drawing her hand down, sliding it beneath the napkin to rest against the bare skin of his chest. It was her turn to feel his heartbeat, his blood coursing at her touch. He took his own hand away and reached out, cupping the back of her neck, drawing her head down until their lips met.

She had always assumed her first kiss would be a chaste peck from a boy nearly as innocent as she was. She had not been ready for this: open-mouthed, passionate, possessive and oh, so delicious. He tasted like oranges and sin and as his tongue moved against hers, she thought of the words he had encouraged her to read: the shedding of clothing and the feel of bodies, skin to skin.

He was nearly naked already, only a sheet covering parts of him that she'd done her best to ignore while caring for him. But Lord help her, she had looked. And she had imagined, was imagining even now. It would be so easy to push the sheet away and stretch out on the bed, giving herself over to her earlier daydream.

She tried to gasp, shocked at the thoughts she was

having, but it only seemed to deepen his kiss. Her hand, which was still trapped between them, pushed ineffectually against his chest, trying to create some space. But he held her fast, his good arm sliding from her neck to stroke her shoulders.

His good arm…

The thought was hazy. The beginnings of a plan.

She slid her hand up his body to the bandage on his shoulder and pressed down.

Now he was the one to gasp, inhaling on a curse and releasing her, his back arched and muscles spasming in pain.

She sat up just as quickly, sliding off the bed and back into the chair beside it, straightening gown and hair before she spoke. 'I am sorry, Your Grace. I did not wish to hurt you.'

'The devil you say,' he muttered through clenched teeth. Then, he smiled. 'But a kiss like that was worth the pain.'

It had been worth the risk of disgrace, as well. If anyone discovered what had happened, that moment of pleasure would be her ruin. Perhaps it was the danger involved that left her blood singing in her veins and her body eager to climb back onto the bed to see what would happen next.

She willed herself to be calm and give him no hint of how it had affected her. It was not as if the act had surprised her. She had known from the moment she had come here that he was a rake and not to be trusted, especially now that he was getting better. He had tried to seduce her and would do so again if she gave him the chance. He would have done the same with any woman foolish enough to be alone with him.

It was her response that was the problem. She had assumed that when the assault on her virtue came, she would be strong enough to resist. But though she had bested him physically, her heart still wanted to give in. If she let this continue, he would use and discard her, just as he had who knew how many others.

What would become of her then?

Being careful to stay out of reach, she walked around the bed and felt amongst the bedclothes to find the fork they had dropped. She placed it in his hand and set the luncheon tray in front of him so he might eat.

Then she walked towards the dressing room.

'Where are you going?'

She turned back to look at him, her face set in the cool, confident smile she used when tending the sick. 'I must attend to a personal matter. As I told you before, you are strong enough to feed yourself. You can manage without me for a few moments, I am sure.'

He stared back at her with an unreadable expression. 'Do not be long.'

'Of course, not.' It was a small lie, but circumstances required it. She allowed herself one last look at him, burning the image into her mind to serve as both keepsake and warning. Then, she turned away, walked into the dressing room and shut the door behind her.

After listening at the door for a moment to be sure he was not following, she stuffed the few items of clothing she'd brought with her into her bag and let herself out through the door at the back of the little room which led to the adjoining suite. From there, it was a short walk to the hall and down the stairs. The only servant she saw was the footman at the front door, who opened it for her without question.

Once outside, she glanced back at the upper windows with a twinge of regret. She had not said a proper goodbye. But it was too late to part as friends. They were more than that, far closer than they should be, if she was honest.

And now, the situation had ended the only way it could have. She was going home. She had achieved what she'd set out to do. Julian would not be a murderer. And Westbridge, her Sebastian, would be fine without her.

* * *

She was gone.

He should never have kissed her. Her response had been willing enough, but there was no sign of experience in it. The goal should have been to pique her curiosity. He'd moved too fast, taken too much pleasure in the feel of her hand on his bare skin, the weight of her body stretched over his, and the sweet taste of her lips.

When she'd put a stop to it, he should have had the sense to apologize. Instead, he'd gloated. He had treated a precious moment as if it was just another conquest. He had fallen back to playing Lothario, too cowardly to reveal the glimpse of his heart that might give her a reason to forgive him.

Then, he'd watched as the heat in her gaze had changed to impersonal courtesy, as if nothing had happened. He might tell himself that it was just a mask for her true feelings. But there had been something final in the look she'd given him as she'd left the room, as if she was closing a door on a part of herself.

He set the lunch tray aside and swung his feet to the floor, ready to go after her. But when he tried to rise, he was overcome by vertigo. He clutched the sheets at his side, waiting for the world to stop rocking, too embarrassed to call out for help.

If he did not hurry, she would get away. But he was equally fearful that she would come back and find him on the carpet in a heap. He wanted her to see him as a man and not some pathetic invalid who needed nothing from her but nursing. He took a few minutes to gather his strength. Then, he inched towards the head of the bed where the bell-pull hung and rang for his valet.

The servant arrived in a moment, surprised to find him alone. 'Where has the nurse gotten to?'

'I could ask you the same question,' Sebastian snapped. 'I am in no condition to look for her. Check the changing room.'

He returned in a moment to say it was empty, just as Sebastian feared it would be. A search of the house proved she had gone, leaving nothing but the Bible resting on the bedside table. The inscription on the end paper revealed that her name was Cassie and that the book had been given by her loving parents, but no more information than that.

He summoned the butler who informed him that she'd arrived without warning on the night of the duel and claimed she'd been sent by the doctor. Given her competence and skill, he'd had no reason to doubt her.

When the doctor arrived, he proclaimed that he was pleased with the progress His Grace had made towards recovery. But he could offer no information as to the identity of his nurse. She had told him she'd been hired by the family.

'I have no family,' Sebastian replied, annoyed with them all. 'All she told me was that her name was Cassie.'

'I have no reason to doubt the fact, Your Grace,' said the doctor. 'But as to anything else about her?' He shrugged.

He called for other servants who might have spoken to her. What of the footmen? The housekeeper? The maids who had tended the room and brought her meals? All of them were equally ignorant of her identity. She'd said nothing of her past or her plans for the future.

'You all allowed a stranger into my bedroom, when I was helpless to protect myself?' he said, incredulous.

There was much shuffling of feet and muttering of apologies from the people assembled. Apparently, that was exactly what had happened.

'Dismissed,' he said, waving his good hand to shoo them away. Then, he pointed to the valet. 'Except for you. I wish to dress.' If no one here could help him, he would have to find her himself.

The valet looked to the doctor, who shrugged

again. 'If hc feels well enough, he can do as he pleases.'

But when they attempted it, it was clear that he was still too infirm to get a shirt over his wounded shoulder. He was trapped in this room for several more days at least. With each minute that passed, Cassie was getting further away and he could do nothing about it.

And whose fault was that?

He should not have kissed her. It had been too soon. He had frightened her away before he'd said the things he needed to say. Even worse, he was not yet sure what he'd meant to declare.

He needed to thank her. When she'd come to him, he was reconciled to death and ready to welcome it. There had been no one left in his life that would miss him should he cease to exist. But she had insisted that he mattered to her. She had wanted him to survive. Her belief in him had changed everything.

How could he reward someone who had both saved his life and renewed his faith in himself? Words were inadequate, and no amount of money would be enough. It was not as if his lovemaking was some sort of fabulous gift rarely bestowed. He was accustomed to taking pleasure wherever and whenever he found it.

But he was not without principles. He did not take

advantage of his staff. There was nothing worse than a supposed gentleman who could not keep his hands off the women in his employ. Cassie had been a temporary member of his household, and he should have treated her with respect.

Instead, he had tried to haul her into bed the minute she'd gotten too close to him. His only defense was that he was unaccustomed to receiving the tenderness she gave so freely as she'd cared for him. He had mistaken the altruism of her profession for an invitation to take liberties.

And yet…

He closed his eyes, remembering the feel of her hands as she'd nursed him. He swore he could remember her lips as well, pressed to his forehead and brushing his ear as she whispered words of encouragement. She felt something for him that was deeper than common kindness. Why else would she have run to save him after hearing he'd been hurt? She'd remained at his side for days, heedless of the impropriety of it. She'd asked for nothing in return. Her only payment had been his recovery.

And that single, delicious kiss. It had frightened her, and she had stopped it before either of them had lost control. But for a few sweet moments, her lips had been warm and willing against his. But there had also been a hesitance to the contact, a sort of untried innocence.

He smiled in amazement as he pieced the clues together. On the lowest night of his life, when he had resigned himself that he was friendless and unloved, a girl had appeared out of nowhere to help him. She was skilled as a nurse, well-spoken, literate and gently mannered. The kiss and her response to it indicated that she was a virgin. Though curious about intimacy, she had no real experience with it. And she had known of his condition the same day it had happened. She must have heard of it by gossip and not from an article in the newspaper.

The pain in his shoulder and the accompanying weakness were forgotten and excitement burned through him like lightning in a summer sky. Somewhere in the city, there was a girl who'd loved him, even as he'd tried to throw his life away. He had not known her. There had been no introduction. But he must have done some good deed for a friend or family member that had earned her unrequited devotion. She'd risked her reputation to save him, but could not resist the single stolen kiss from the man she secretly adored.

There was an impediment to a proper courtship, just as in any great love story. She might be of poor and humble birth, far beneath him socially.

She might be engaged. Her father might disapprove of him.

He laughed. If he was honest, most of London disapproved of him. Or at least they had until today. Now that he had found the woman who would be his future, his rakish days were behind him. He would prove to his mysterious Cassie that her faith in him was not misplaced. She had given him a second chance at life. He would use it to become a better man.

First, he must get out of this damned sick bed and into a decent suit of clothes. Then, he would track her down and apologize for his clumsy attempt at seduction. He would court her properly, laying his title, his wealth and his heart at her feet. Their wedding would be the talk of the *ton*, the standard by which all other ceremonies were measured. And so would be their union, filled with laughter and children and pleasure she had not yet imagined.

He had but to find her and explain.

Chapter Four

One year later

Sebastian sat in his usual chair at White's, enjoying a morning coffee, with nothing to look forward to but another idle day in London. He picked up the copy of *The Times* waiting on the table beside him, giving the headlines his usual, cursory viewing. Then the gossip columns. And finally, when he was sure that no one was observing him, he moved on to the personal column to be sure that his ad still ran.

> Cassie: I have nothing but regret for the unfortunate way we parted. If you can find it in your heart to forgive me, write to me at my London address. Ease my suffering and all that I am shall be yours. W

There had been no response in all the months that had passed. But neither had there been any communication that would make him stop searching. When he'd recovered, he'd checked every hospital and private agency that supplied nurses and found no sign of her. He'd searched church rolls and school rosters, and made discreet inquiries amongst the merchants and cits looking for one who might have had business dealings with him and had an unmarried daughter. It had all been for naught. It seemed she'd appeared on his doorstep, out of nowhere, and returned to oblivion when she'd left him.

If he was of a more fanciful nature, he might have convinced himself that hers had been a truly angelic intervention and not a metaphorical one. The effect she'd had on him was nothing short of miraculous, healing his physical wounds and cutting through the dark fog that had enveloped his soul.

But angels gave blessings, not kisses. The woman he'd held was flesh and hot blood, and living in London. It was a large city, but not infinite. He would find her. Hope renewed, he set the paper aside and smiled, reliving the one kiss they'd shared and thinking of the ones to come.

'What are you smiling at?' Septon took the seat at his side and took the paper up again. 'Have you done something worthy of recording in the tattle sheets?'

'Nothing interesting,' he replied, giving his friend a chilly nod of greeting. 'My conscience is clean and has been for some time.' Not that anyone had noticed. Compared to the dastard he'd been a year ago, he was practically a monk. At least Septon should give him some credit. Hadn't he apologized for provoking their duel and forgiven the fellow for nearly killing him? Sebastian had been most magnanimous about the matter. They'd made up and were best friends again.

But now that he had married and had given up his own rakish ways, Septon seemed oblivious to anything but his own happiness. The few times Sebastian had seen him out in the evenings, he was accompanied by his wife, Portia. They flirted shamelessly with each other in public and left gatherings early and together as if they could not wait to be alone.

It was disgusting.

Now he was scanning down the same gossip column that Sebastian had perused, looking for himself. 'I am just making sure that there is proper mention of the come-out ball for my sister,' he said with a satisfied nod.

'Notifying the world to know she is on the market?' Sebastian replied, arching his eyebrow. 'Why don't you just take her to Tattersalls and call the auctioneer?'

Septon responded with an equally cynical smile.

'Because I love my sister and mean to treat her better than horseflesh. Although an auction would sort the fortune hunters out of the pack and save the hundreds of pounds that I've spent on the trappings of the Season. She is a very sensible girl and does not ask for much. But if this is to be done, I wish for it to be done well.'

Sebastian nodded in acknowledgement. Julian had only recently discovered his illegitimate sister, hidden in the country. To make up for his father's neglect of her, he was taking great pains to see that she married well.

Now he was running his finger down the newspaper column, stopping on an item to give the paper an approving tap. 'They've made a proper mention of the school we are raising funds for. It is to be both a charity event and her come-out ball. I have made her adoptive father, the Reverend Fisk, a headmaster there.'

'That simply reeks of virtue,' Sebastian said, giving a small shudder and making no effort to hide the sarcasm in his voice.

'It was Portia's idea,' Septon replied, oblivious to the jibe. 'She wishes the *ton* to focus on my sister's proper upbringing and not the misfortune of her birth. She has remade me, as well. I am an upstanding member of the peerage now, and not the rakehell I was a year ago.'

'Well done, you,' he replied, wishing his coffee were something stronger.

'I cannot recommend marriage enough. It has made me a new man.'

Sebastian was tempted to reply that horses were tamed after gelding. But since Septon was not yet expecting an heir, it might not have been well received. Instead, he said, 'And this ball you speak of, it is tonight, is it not?'

'Indeed,' Septon said. 'We have had to rent an assembly room for the evening. Portia is seeing to the decorations as we speak.'

'I only mention it because I have not yet received an invitation,' he replied.

This was followed by a pause that embarrassed them both. Then, Septon said, 'We did not think you would be interested. It is going to be deadly dull. Such things usually are. You have complained about them in the past, you know.'

'Indeed.' A year ago, they had mocked such gatherings together. But things had changed for both of them, and it was another sign that his friend had not noticed the improvement in him.

'You are welcome to attend, of course,' Septon added.

But not to meet your sister.

Again, Sebastian was tempted to speak. He could remind his friend that the girl was a half-sister and born on the wrong side of the blanket. He was a duke, and more than a prime catch for the most eligible girls in England and far out of the reach of a by-blow, even if she was spawned by a peer and raised by a vicar.

But that would ignore the unfortunate truth: they had spent too many evenings steeped in debauchery for Septon to have any illusions about Sebastian's character. He would never be an ideal match for a friend's sister, no matter his rank or recent good behaviour. He had far too much past to forgive.

It hurt. But not overmuch. He had no intention of marrying Septon's sister, so it hardly mattered. 'Perhaps I shall pay my respects,' he said with a neutral smile, setting aside his cup and rising to leave. Then, he could not help but add, 'Tell the girl to save me a dance.'

'Of course,' Julian said with a nod, returning to his paper and probably hoping that Sebastian would forget the whole thing.

At seven thirty that evening, Cassie stood on the edge of the hired assembly hall in Argyle Street ready to make her debut. Portia had been planning the evening since the end of last year and had reserved the rooms and chosen the date so the ball would be the first major event of the Season and impossible to ignore.

Invitations were sent to the best and the brightest of London Society and some two hundred people had responded, eager to see and be seen supporting the Duke's charity and gaining introduction to the elusive Miss Fisk.

Cassie had been in London for a year and a half now, but few people knew of the fact. While she had not exactly been in seclusion, they had decided between them that it would be better to put off the formal introduction to the *ton* until the following year, when the most eligible men had returned to London for Parliament's new session.

It had worked for the best, since her poor brother had had no idea how to go out preparing her for a Season and would have been close to useless last year. His sudden marriage after the duel had solved so many problems. Portia had handled everything, from polishing the scandal off the Septon title to decorating the hall for this ball.

She had even helped with Cassie's wardrobe, coming with her to pick fabrics and styles for the many new gowns. Then, she had sent to the country house for family jewellery that would best accent them.

Tonight, Cassie wore amethysts that had been in the entail for generations, a quiet reminder to those who recognized them that she was an acknowledged member of the family.

The evening was perfect. Really it was. Everything a girl could dream of.

If one was still a girl, perhaps. At six and twenty, Cassie stretched the definition of the word. And, if one had ever imagined a formal London Season, which Cassie had not.

It was not that she was ungrateful. Julian and Portia wanted what was best for her. They offered more than the Fisks, her loving mother and father, could ever provide. But she had long ago resigned herself to not having fine clothes or jewels, or the attention of wealthy and powerful suitors. She did not need any of these things to be happy.

She had not even needed to know her true family, although it was nice to have a brother, especially one who loved her, as Julian did. She had reconciled herself to having the simple life she'd had in the rectory with the Fisks.

She had never imagined a night such as this. The sconces and tables were festooned with heliotropes. The tables in the dining room were stacked with delicacies. The chandeliers sparkled, as did the wine glasses and the champagne in them.

The people would sparkle, as well. The guests would be titled gentlemen and their ladies, would be decked in silk and sheer muslin, their throats dripping with jewels. And all of them would be watching her. Judging her. Whispering behind their fans about her.

For a moment, she was overcome with panic and stared around her, looking for escape. But before she could run, her father and her mother were at her side, offering her hugs of assurance and congratulations.

As her mother leaned in to kiss her, she whispered, 'You needn't be frightened, dear. The Duke and Duchess have taken care of you so far. They will not abandon you now.'

'But what if…' She looked around to be sure no one could hear her. 'What if I don't want to get married?'

Her mother pulled away and looked back at her, surprised. 'It is rather the point of a Season, Cassandra. When the Duke took you to London, we all assumed that he would find you a husband.'

'I am aware of that,' she whispered back. 'But…' She gave her father an apologetic smile. 'At the time, no one ever asked me about it. Everyone just assumed. I assumed, as well. And now?' She waved her hands at her surroundings. 'Here we are.'

Her father patted her hand. 'It is not as if you will

be forced against your will to wed a man you do not like. But when you did not find a husband in the parish, we thought a wider pool of suitors might help you find someone you liked.'

'Perhaps,' she said, hoping it would make him feel better. But she did not think he understood at all. She had gone from her father's house, to the house in St John's Wood. There, she had lived just as she wanted for eighteen months. It had been lovely, just as it was. She wanted freedom and independence. But she did not know if Julian would support her forever, should she refuse to marry.

'I could be useful,' she said, staring at the doorway of the room, where the first guests had started to arrive. 'I could be a governess, or a nurse, perhaps.'

Her father gave her a sad smile. 'That would have been a decent plan, had you continued to live as our daughter. But a Duke's sister does not need employment.'

He meant that it would be an embarrassment to Julian, she supposed. The women in the families of great men were destined to marry other great men. They were not supposed to shun the honour and seek employment. Perhaps it would have been better, had he never found her.

Her mother gave her another kiss, then turned her

and gave her a gentle push in the direction of the door. 'Go and meet your guests. And do not worry so. Everything will be fine.'

'Your brother will help you to choose an honourable man,' her father added. 'Someone who will allow you to do the good works you wish to, but who will keep you in love and comfort.'

'As you wish, Papa,' she said, doing her best to smile and pretend that all was well. Perhaps she should speak to Julian or Portia about her concerns. They would probably remind her that a woman with a job was little better than a servant, at the beck and call of whoever employed her. But a job was something that one could walk away from, if it did not suit.

Marriage was another matter entirely. It was until death. It said so, right in the vows. Once she said the words, there would be no turning back. And never, in twenty-six years, had she met a man she wanted to give her forever to.

At least not to the sort that her father might approve of. It was probably a sign of a weak character that the only man she'd ever been interested in was a wastrel. She had attached far too much importance to a single kiss. It was a foolish act that had raised equally foolish fantasies.

If she was to meet the man now?

Well, she simply wouldn't. Not tonight, at least. She'd made sure he wasn't on the guest list. She might see him eventually, but she doubted he would even recognize her. Men like that did not really look at the women who served them. To see her again, dressed properly, would be like seeing an entirely different person.

If he remembered his nurse at all. He had likely given the credit for his recovery to a good doctor and a strong constitution.

But she remembered each minute she'd spent with him, far too well. Some nights, when she was alone in bed, she swore she could feel the heat of his fevered skin. The shape of his body. The softness of his hair as she'd brushed it out of his face. And, of course, his lips.

None of which she should be thinking about now. She took her place with Julian and Portia near the door, ready to be introduced to a flock of men who had many good qualities to recommend them and reputations that were not nearly as roguish as the Duke of Westbridge. Perhaps one of them would help her forget. It would only take one.

Each eligible man that passed her began by speaking with Julian, assuring him of their support for the school he was funding, then turned to her and requested a dance. As she let them scrawl their names on the card tied to her wrist, she tried to commit the snippets of conversation to memory, as a way to rank them against each other.

A few were vulgar enough to set an amount on their promised donations. She rejected them out of hand. She hoped this was not some auction where Julian meant to pass ownership of her to the highest bidder.

Personally, she gave the greatest favour to a young man named Tobias Blake who was reading for the clergy and could promise nothing but his assistance in teaching and mentoring the impoverished orphans Julian meant to educate. Mr Blake was visually unprepossessing and seemed rather more interested in the school than he did her. But she could not fault his earnestness.

Her father would approve. But should that be her primary goal? While she wished to be guided by his wisdom, she had hoped that she would feel something more than vague approval when looking at her future husband.

A little later, a man passed who was likely Julian's favourite. He and Lord Andrew Rutland talked for some time, mostly about the man's father, who was an earl and an ally of her brother's in Parliament. Lord Rutland was well-spoken, well-tailored and probably ambitious. She suspected he wanted something from Julian and thought the shortest route to his approval might run through her heart.

Or perhaps over it. He had a pleasant smile, but she was not sure she fully trusted him. Still, she did not hesitate when he offered to partner her in a reel. It would not do to refuse too many candidates before giving them some sort of hearing. And, if this one made Julian happy?

Then, perhaps Julian should marry him.

She thrust that thought aside as unworthy. Her brother had done so much for her that she owed it to him to be polite to his friends. And really, there was nothing so very wrong with Lord Rutland. He might have altruistic reasons for wanting a peer's favour. If he meant to help orphans, as Julian was doing, she could be of help.

She turned to watch him go while Portia greeted the next man in line. 'We did not expect to see you this evening, Your Grace.' Her tone as she greeted this guest seemed strange, as if her courtesy was only superficial.

'I imagine you did not. But Septon speaks so persuasively about the school he is sponsoring that I could not fail to show my support.'

She did not need to turn and look to know him. That smooth voice had haunted her dreams for months. She turned back slowly, and by the time she faced him, her composure was firmly in place and she could greet him as a stranger.

Their eyes met, and she abandoned any hope that he might have forgotten her. The change in him was subtle, but plain to her. A slight elevation of an eyebrow and dilation of the pupils. An infinitesimal hitch in his breath.

And then, he turned back to Julian as if nothing had changed. 'What was the cause again, Septon? Wayward girls?' The question was like a knife wrapped in cotton wool. Soft and innocent on the outside, but sharp underneath.

'Orphans,' said Julian. 'Boys.' He was smiling as Westbridge was, but obviously annoyed.

And now, the Duke turned to her, still smiling, still sly. 'And this must be your long-lost sister.'

'May I present Miss Cassandra Fisk. The Duke of Westbridge.'

'Your Grace,' she said automatically and curtsied. She kept her eyes lowered. She had seen enough in the brief look they'd shared. He was every bit as handsome as he had been, when she'd nursed him. More so, now that he was healthy. The colour had returned to his face and he'd lost that gaunt look from too many days without food.

And just as it had a year ago, her heart beat a little faster and her skin felt flushed. She was tempted to fan herself and complain of the heat. But that would only call attention to her condition and prolong the meeting.

'Delighted to meet you, Miss Fisk.' He did not seem to be experiencing any difficulties at all. His voice was smooth as he took her hand raising it to his lips and kissing the air above it.

'And you, Your Grace,' she replied, sure that she could feel the heat of his breath through her glove. 'My brother speaks of you, often.'

'He has told me surprisingly little about you,' he said with just a hint of acid. 'But now that we have met, I look forward to knowing you better.'

What was she to say to that? The temptation was to announce that he knew her quite well enough. Or perhaps, she should simply run.

Then, she remembered that there was nothing to be afraid of. If he'd meant to expose their previous relationship, he would have said something already. This might be the only time she would speak with him, no matter what he'd just said. Her brother would never approve of an acquaintance between them. The Duke's reputation was far too rackety.

Nor would he wish to waste time on her. He was a notorious bachelor and likely came here to support Julian, not because he was seeking a wife. Even if he meant to marry this Season, he would not consider someone who could not even name her mother. She need only follow her original plan. She would be polite and deny, deny, deny.

'Thank you. You are too kind.' She glanced towards the dance floor. 'But now, I fear, you must excuse me. The dancing is beginning and I am obligated.'

He looked down at her dance card. 'Is there a space left for me?'

'I fear not,' she said with an apologetic smile.

He caught the card in his hand. 'But wait. A single blank line for a country dance.' He reached for the little pencil. 'Set to "The Happy Return". A lovely tune, is it not?'

'I do not know it,' she said firmly.

'You will catch on quick enough, I am sure.' And then, he winked and walked away.

After he left his hosts, Sebastian walked to the refreshment table and accepted a glass of champagne from the waiter there. He pretended to focus on the drink in his hand, holding it up to the light and peering past it at the dance floor where the guest of honour was dancing.

Could it be coincidence? Could she have a twin? Perhaps he had been so addled by the fever during his recovery that he'd not gotten a proper look at his nurse and was imagining a resemblance.

No on all counts. It was her. He was sure of it. Two women might look similar, by accident or blood relation. But they would not share the name. His Cassie, and Septon's sister were one and the same.

He had searched for her for a year, and she'd been under his nose the whole time. He had lain awake nights, imagining the moment of rediscovery where he could apologize and tell her of the changes he'd made in his character to earn a second chance. God help him, he had been celibate for her, which could not have been healthy for him.

And she had obviously not given him a thought in the whole of the time. She had looked at him just now as if she'd never seen him in her life. Could it be amnesia of some kind? Had she nursed, kissed and abandoned so many men that he was forgotten in the crowd?

Or was she feigning ignorance in hope that he would go away and leave her alone?

If so, she was bound for disappointment. He had a good mind to storm out onto the floor, pull her away from her partner and demand an explanation, right now.

He took another sip of wine to cool his temper. It was not as if she could admit to knowing him in front of her brother. Nor would it do for him to publicly disgrace her while attempting to get an acknowledgement. If someone heard him announce that the last time they'd spoken was in his bedroom, unfortunate conclusions would be drawn. They'd be forced to marry immediately.

It was not as if he objected to marrying her. It had been his plan for months. But he wanted it to happen on his terms and after the courtship she deserved. He did not want to see yet another scandal attached to his name, or hers splashed across the gossip columns.

There was also the matter of her brother. He glanced in Septon's direction, raising his glass to show he was enjoying the party, and not thinking about despoiling the fellow's sister. He had known there was something keeping them apart. Julian was a formidable obstacle.

It was something the man would have to accept eventually. But tonight was far too soon.

So he had another drink, smiling and nodding, making polite chit-chat with the other guests, waiting out the time until his turn to dance arrived. Then, he set his glass aside and strolled towards her, giving no outward sign that he had been anticipating this moment for months. Arriving at her side, he bowed deeply and offered his hand. 'Miss Fisk.' He smiled. 'Or may I call you Cassie?'

She looked baffled for a moment, as if she had not recognized her own name.

'Your friends call you Cassie, do they not?' He winked.

If he was expecting a knowing look in return, he did not get it. She was still looking at him with a polite smile, as if wondering what he was suggesting by winking at her. Then she said, 'I am sorry. Is there something in your eye?'

'Perhaps,' he said, reaching into his pocket for a handkerchief. He dabbed it briefly and tucked the cloth away again. 'And now, let us take our places before the music starts. We would not want to miss the opportunity.'

'I am sure there shall be others,' she said with the same, distant courtesy. 'You are a duke, and on the guest lists of many people here in London. I doubt I shall be able to avoid you.'

'Do you wish to?' he said, taking her hand and leading her to her place in the set.

'It is common knowledge that you are a rake,' she said. 'And not to be trusted in the company of ladies.'

He gave her an approving nod. 'It makes one wonder why a gently bred girl would come into my house of her own free will.' Then, he favoured her with a direct stare, waiting for the answer.

'I cannot imagine a reason,' she said, staring back at him with a faintly confused expression.

He had to hide his disappointment. It had been the perfect opportunity for her to offer a sly comment, an answering wink, or at least a change in smile to indicate their shared past. There had been nothing.

'Let us dance, shall we?' he said as the music began, offering a bow to her curtsy. It was a country dance and hardly intimate, but when they crossed each other, touching hands and circling, there were moments of shared intimacy. As they passed each other at the centre, he murmured, 'It is a shame we could not share a waltz.'

He walked through the next steps, waiting until they met again for an answer. 'Thank you, but I do not know if I will be allowed that dance,' she said. Then, she was gone again.

'Surely, you will not be so deprived,' he responded on the next pass.

'My brother is very strict,' she said as they took hands and proceeded down the centre.

He had a good mind to tell her what he knew of her brother from days past. Septon might be proper now, but he'd been a devil with the ladies just a year ago. 'I will chide him for being such a prig, and we shall have that dance.' He squeezed her hand and they parted again.

As she turned back to him, she raised her eyebrows in surprise but said nothing.

The dance continued in silence and ended with them bowing and curtsying to each other amid polite applause for the orchestra. He could feel the opportunity to speak slipping away as he walked her back to her place at the side of the dance floor. With each step, the tension grew in him, and annoyance as well, that he could feel no answering emotion from her. Where was the devotion that had drawn her to him, last year? Finally, he blurted, 'You needn't keep up the charade.'

'I beg your pardon?' She tipped her head, looking not at him but through him, her mind already on her next partner.

'Last year,' he said, waving a hand in front of her face to regain her attention. 'In my bedroom.'

She took a step back, mortified. *'I beg your pardon?'*

'After the duel,' he whispered, waiting for her to break.

She did not, continuing to stare at him. At last, she frowned and said, 'I was under the impression that you had forgiven my brother for what had happened.'

'I have,' he said.

'Then please refrain from—' she gave a little wave of her hand '—whatever it is that you are attempting here.' And then, the next gentleman arrived to claim his dance and she walked away without another look.

Chapter Five

The sun was already peeking over the horizon as they rode back to the Septon townhouse, where Cassie would be staying for the Season. Her parents had left for their rooms there at just past midnight, declaring the hours of London parties to be quite beyond them.

It did feel rather decadent to dance all night and sleep through the morning. But apparently, it was the way things were done in the *ton*, and she would have to get used to it. Still, it might have been easier to be going home to her own house. She had much to think about and wished she could do it in privacy.

'Did you enjoy the ball?' Portia must have noticed her distraction and was eager for reassurance.

Cassie forced herself to smile. 'Very much so. Thank you so much for all you have done for me.' It was a mostly truthful response. It had been lovely until Sebastian had arrived. After that, she'd spent the rest of the evening fearing he might announce to all who would listen that they already knew each other far too well.

If he did, she would deny it. No one would believe him, she was sure. But the thought made her heart race.

Or was that simply from being in the same room with him again? It had been a year, and she still remembered his kiss as if it had happened tonight. The dance they'd shared had been wonderful, even if it had not been a waltz. It had been an excuse to hold his hand, even briefly, and she had enjoyed it more than she should have. But then, he had pressed her to admit that she knew him. She had denied it, of course. There was no way she could explain what had happened to Julian without creating some kind of scandal.

She feared Sebastian must see at first glance that she was lying. But when they had parted, she'd seen doubt in his eyes, as if he was not sure his memory was true. Perhaps, in another meeting or two, he would be convinced that he was mistaken.

She should not be disappointed at the thought, but she was.

'I had not expected to see Westbridge, tonight.' This was from Portia, again, directed to Julian. But

Cassie had to stifle her reaction, for it felt as if her sister-in-law could read her mind.

'He caught me at the club, today, asking why he had not been invited,' Julian said from the other side of the carriage. 'I could not very well tell him the truth.'

'Perhaps that was exactly what he needed to hear,' Portia said a little primly. 'A come-out ball for an innocent young lady is the last place he belongs.'

In the dark, Cassie smiled. In truth, Portia was younger than she was. But the fact that she was married gave her authority that Cassie had yet to earn.

'He did not upset you, I trust,' Portia said, turning to her.

'We danced,' Cassie confirmed. 'There was nothing exceptional about it.'

'That is good to know.' Portia gave her an approving nod.

'You were the only one he danced with,' Julian said, his tone pensive.

'I had not noticed,' Cassie replied, trying to ignore the rush of excitement she felt to know he had not come there to see anyone else.

'How does he usually behave at events like this?' Portia said, giving her husband a stern look.

'He does not normally attend such things,' Julian said, still thoughtful. 'But it is quite possible that he came to this one simply because he was not invited. He is a contrary reprobate, after all.' His brow furrowed. 'But if he bothered to insert himself in a place where he was not welcome, it makes sense that he would dance with the guest of honour. He would want to call attention to his presence.'

'I suppose it was a vain hope that you would not meet him at all,' Portia said.

'Is he really so dangerous?' Cassie asked, unable to contain her curiosity.

'I don't know if *dangerous* is the right word,' Julian said, scuffing his boot against the floor. 'I have never known him to ruin a woman who was not already…' He cleared his throat. 'Who was not willing,' he finished. 'Married, or widowed, or in the demimondaine. His lov…' He cleared his throat again. 'His female acquaintances have all been as experienced as he is.'

Cassie suppressed a giggle. 'You needn't be so careful with me, Julian. I am old enough to know that men sometimes take advantage when an opportunity presents itself. But if he does not bother with virgins, I should be safe enough.'

'We do not want him to associate with you, all the same,' Portia added. 'He is a drunkard and a gambler and keeps all sorts of low company. When he does finally marry, I pity the poor girl he chooses for I doubt he will come home to her one night in ten.'

'That would be very unpleasant,' Cassie agreed. The last thing she wanted was a husband who would only abandon her, as her true parents had done.

'If you encourage him or his ilk, it will only lead to trouble. We want you to present your best face to the *ton* and do not want to give the gossips a reason to talk.'

Because of her illegitimacy, Cassie supposed. To a certain extent, people would look the other way because of the identity of her father and the fact that the family was acknowledging her, even though the old Duke hadn't. But they might still wonder about her mother and think that some taint of indiscretion had been passed down to the daughter. A quarter of a century spent with the Fisks would mean nothing to such people.

It was not fair. She had done nothing wrong.

Well, almost nothing. One kiss should not matter. Even if it had been with a rake.

On a bed.

With thoughts like that, perhaps there was some trace of impropriety that had been passed to her by blood. If she wished to make a good marriage, she would need to be even more proper than the other girls out this Season. There must be no gossip at all. 'I will be careful,' she promised, thinking of how much easier it had been in the country, when no one had cared where she went or what she did. Then, she had been prepared for benign spinsterhood. And now? Whether she liked it or not, she was to be a lady.

They arrived at the townhouse and Julian helped them down from the carriage and ushered them into the house. Cassie went up to the room that had been allotted to her, with her adopted parents on one side and Julian and Portia on the other. Though her family had been content for her to live alone for months, suddenly she could not be trusted to sleep unless she was properly chaperoned at all times.

She let out a little breath of frustration. She missed the freedom of living on her own, even if it hadn't been quite proper. Then, she closed the door of her room, where her maid, Bessie, was already bustling around, preparing her dressing gown and nightclothes. Someone had placed a crystal vase filled with lilacs on the dressing table. Their perfume was heavy in the night air.

She looked to Bessie for explanation. She had seen no lilacs near her brother's home. Perhaps they were left over from the decorations for the ball, though she could not remember seeing them there, either.

'Where did these lovely flowers come from?' She bent low over the blooms and inhaled their scent.

'A man stopped at the door, an hour or so ago. He said they was for you,' the girl replied.

'How strange.' Most anyone in London would have known she was away from the house tonight. The ball had been mentioned in all the newspapers. Even if they had not known of it, why would they come so early in the morning? 'Did he leave a name?'

'No, miss.'

'Was there a card?'

'No, miss.'

As Bessie went about the business of preparing her for bed, Cassie stared at the blooms in the little vase, wondering about the man who'd brought them. She'd met so many men this evening, but none had given her the impression that they might want to gift her with flowers at such a late hour.

Well, perhaps one…

She swallowed, fighting the urge to smile. If it was the Duke, it was an unwelcome intrusion. As Portia had reminded her, men like him were full of empty promises and she would be a fool to trust anything he did.

Of course, Julian had been as bad as Westbridge a year ago. She'd loved him then, and she loved him just as much now that marriage had reformed him. His behaviour since marriage disproved Portia's warning that rakes could not be trusted. It was a wonder she did not notice the fact.

Cassie closed her eyes and swallowed again, then opened them, trying to look at the flowers without emotion. She should not be thinking of marriage in the same sentence as Westbridge. She knew from experience that if they were alone, he would take any liberty he could get away with.

To pick a blossom on his way home and drop it at her door was hardly a Herculean task. It had cost him nothing. It was not a dozen roses, or orchids straight from a hothouse. It was probably a theft from someone else's garden.

It was also nearly six in the morning. Low-hanging lilacs were the only flowers available at this hour. If a man was walking home and thinking fondly of someone he'd shared a dance with, he might be motivated to pluck a bloom or two. It was rather romantic, really.

And foolish of her to build a fantasy on them. She did not even know if it was the Duke. Tomorrow she would receive a call from one of the dozens of gentlemen she'd danced with, and he would ask shyly if she had liked the flowers. Convinced of this, she picked a single blossom from the cone and pinched it between her fingers, carrying it to bed with her so the scent of it could follow her into dreams.

Sebastian woke at noon the next day; with a sense of purpose he'd not felt in months. He had found the woman who had haunted his dreams for almost a year. He had talked to her, danced with her. And, after drinking far too much champagne, he had wandered past her house and left her a nosegay like the lovesick swain he was.

This morning, or rather this afternoon, he must decide what was to come next. Until last night, he had imagined no difficulties in winning the mysterious Cassie's affections. She already had a fondness for him. Why else would she have wanted to save him? He had looks, wealth, and power and would offer them all to her, and the job would be done.

He could not dazzle Cassandra Fisk so easily. She was not exactly rich and titled, but her brother was. She had likely learned of Sebastian through Septon. Perhaps she had become curious about him after some amusing anecdote. The curiosity had grown into a *tendre*. Word of his injury and fear of his death had caused her to rush to his side…

He sighed. Sometime soon, he would worm the story out of her. He could imagine them naked in bed, her head resting on his chest as she shyly admitted the origins of her fascination.

He rang for his breakfast tray, still smiling. There would be time later to fulfill those fantasies. For now? She was pretending she had never met him. He blamed Julian for this. The fellow had been pouring poison in her ears, promising her a Season that would end with her tied to someone safe and boring, honourable but unexceptional.

She deserved better. Excitement. Adventure. Romance. She would be a duchess. His duchess. It might require a bit of persuading to return her to the love-struck girl she'd been last year. But once she realized the change her devotion had made in him, the flame in her would be rekindled. He would light it off the fire in his own heart, which had grown in those months apart from the sparks of lust she'd seen to the steady glow of love.

She would laugh when she learned how sentimental he'd become. It made him laugh, as well. His heart was lighter than it had been in ages. There had been so much grief in his life, and so many dashed hopes and disappointments. His father had been a rock. His grandmother, an anchor. Without them, he had drifted, lost and alone.

But Cassie's arrival at his bedside had changed

all that. She had given him her love. Now he would return it, a hundredfold.

At least, he would once a few small difficulties had been cleared away.

The butler arrived with his eggs and Sebastian reached for the napkin. 'Barnes,' he said with a magnanimous smile. 'Get me the morning papers, the invitations from the post and my appointment book.'

The butler gave him a baffled look. 'You want the news, and the mail? With breakfast?'

Sebastian sighed. 'Do I need to repeat the request? I must see the scandal sheets, immediately.'

'You are not usually interested in such things, Your Grace.'

'That was the old me, Barnes. Today, I am very interested in what the *ton* is up to. And who would I talk to about getting some vouchers for Almack's? Or do I have them already? Dammit man, search the study. I am sure I have some unanswered mail there. Bring it immediately.'

'You mean to answer your mail, Your Grace?' Barnes blinked.

'I cannot simply arrive at gatherings with no notice,' he said. 'At least, not anymore. This Season, I must have a plan.'

'Very well, Your Grace,' the butler said with a slight shake of his head, as if to say he would obey but doubted that the change would be permanent. Then, he stepped out of the room and closed the door.

By the time he had finished his coffee, Barnes had reappeared with a basket of unanswered invitations, *The Post*, *The Chronical* and *The Times* and several back issues found in the kitchen firebox. On the top of the stack was the calendar he'd been using to record important appointments.

At least, he should have done. There hadn't been an entry since Christmas. But there was no time like the present to reform his social habits, which were lagging behind the other reforms to his character. So he opened it to the current month and began sorting his mail by date.

After an hour of perusal, cross-referencing newspaper articles with announcements and sorting things by date, he had a fair idea of the gatherings that might invite Septon and his sister and had found the corresponding invitations in his basket.

He did not usually attend the sorts of events where young ladies were found, though he was always invited to them. Hostesses might disapprove of him in private, but he was an unmarried peer and a prized catch on any guest list. While they might not want him marrying their daughter, he was bound to marry someone eventually and they did not want to miss his fall when it occurred.

There was no better place to be seen than Almack's. After much searching, Barnes discovered his voucher being used as a bookmark in a volume of French poetry. He had two days to prepare for the weekly ball, more than enough time to trim his hair, polish the buckles on his knee breeches and practice the apology that he had been planning since she'd run away.

The place was deadly and he had not been there in ages. But, as he had told Barnes, this year would be different. Cassie was sure to be there. So would he. Last night, she had denied him. But in the days to come, she would see him again and again. Some night, he would get her away from her chaperones so she could admit her feelings for him. He would offer his heart and his body. Or his body and his heart, if she were amenable and he could manage to seduce her uninterrupted. Self-denial was not his strong point. And was it really necessary, if the ceremony followed in short order?

The valet appeared, glanced at the scattered papers on the bed and desk, then went back to the job of preparing his shave.

Another doubter.

Sebastian smiled at him, his good mood undiminished. This was the first day of his new life. With time and the love of Cassandra Fisk, the world would see the man he could become.

It was Wednesday night, and Bessie was putting the finishing touches on Cassie's hair, securing the bun with pearl-headed pins and curling the front and sides so they would frame her face as she danced. To finish, she anchored a pearl diadem atop her head that would match the pearl necklace Cassie already wore. Her gown was heavily embroidered white muslin, accented with spangles and even more pearls.

Cassie stood and stared at herself in the mirror. So much white. White was the height of fashion this year. It made her feel cool and untouchable, like a column in a Greek temple. If she was still longing for a flash of colour? It proved how out of step she was with the ladies of London.

Tonight, of all nights, she did not want to bring notice to herself for the wrong reasons. She would be mixing with a crowd even more select than the one that had attended her ball. Stories of Almack's had reached her, even when she'd lived in the country, chiefly that it would be impossible for a girl like herself to gain admittance. The patronesses accepted only the most suitable men for the most high-born ladies. Their lists would never include a country miss with no wealth or pedigree.

But it seemed, when one was the sister of a duke, no matter how shadowed one's past might be, all doors opened. She took a deep breath to settle her nerves. She was rather long in the tooth for a place like Almack's. She had been practically on the shelf when she'd lived in Natters Mill, while many of the girls she would meet tonight were six years younger and already in their second Season.

Of course, they were not the sisters of a duke. Especially not one as generous as Julian was. He had assured her that there was nothing to fear. He wanted her to enjoy herself. He would not force her into a union for the sake of political or financial connection. The choice of whom to marry, or whether to marry at all, would be hers.

Assuming she chose well, of course. She glanced to her journal, with the lilac spear pressed between the pages. No one had stepped forward to announce themselves as the giver, which left her with her first, unproved suspicion. What an unwise choice that would be if it were true.

A thrill went through her at the thought of the Duke, but she was unsure whether it was fear or excitement. When she had tended him, she hadn't considered what would happen after. She should have realized that with the acquaintance between him and Julian, they would be bound to meet again.

But probably not tonight. Almack's was for husband hunting, and for men who were thinking of the future and didn't mind being prey. Sebastian Morehead was not the sort to fall into an obvious trap.

Neither would she see Mr Blake, who was poor and lacked connections to gain admittance. Nor would she see her parents, who had returned home. But not until they'd shared tea with the serious young clergyman when he had visited her the morning after the ball. He'd spoken most earnestly about his plans to settle in the country if he could find a living.

Her father had declared it a sound plan and remarked that he must marry and start a family in short order, as a wife and children were an asset that must not be overlooked when seeking a parish.

Then, everyone had looked to her.

She had agreed and nodded approvingly, hoping he was not assuming she would accept him on so little acquaintance. He was nice enough, and very sincere. But when she talked to him, she felt nothing stronger than nebulous admiration. She was most relieved when he suggested a visit to the Royal Menagerie in the coming week. It would give them a chance to speak of something other than his aspirations to give her more of the life she'd already had.

Tonight, she would associate with the polar opposite of the young clergyman. The men who danced with her would be offering her a life of idleness and privilege. They would have one house in the country and another in town, tenants, servants and all the other trappings of wealth.

Such things would be nice. But she'd much rather be excited by the spirit of the man who held them than the material goods themselves. The men she'd spoken to thus far had acted as if she was not so much a person as another item that could be added to the inventory of their successes. Was it too much to wish for a man who wished to hear of her hopes and dreams, so they might choose a future that pleased them both?

Perhaps tonight she would meet such a person. After a final glance in the mirror, she went down the stairs to where Julian and Portia waited for her in the foyer. Her brother offered an arm to each of them and they went out to the carriage for the ride to King Street.

When they arrived at the assembly hall, he helped them down from the carriage and escorted them again into the ballroom, looking more stiff and formal than she had ever seen him. He was arrayed in knee breeches and a black evening coat, as were all the other men there, a stark contrast to the many white muslin dresses, the sparkle of jewels and the few splashes of colour from the gowns of the bravest ladies.

'It is splendid, is it not?' Portia said leaning close to whisper to her. 'I was not here often. My mother and I lost the vouchers before I could finish my Season. But I enjoyed the few visits I had.'

Cassie nodded back at her, too awed to speak.

'Now that we are here, you are free to do as you like.'

'Really?' she said, giving her sister-in-law a doubtful smile.

'Within reason of course,' Portia said stifling a laugh. 'Tonight, Julian and I will not be watching over you like hawks over a chick. We will not have to. The patronesses will do so for us.'

'Are they really so strict?'

'Very,' Portia assured her. 'You will not be allowed to waltz until they give you permission. They will choose your partners as well and see to all the introductions.'

'How comforting,' Cassie said, bidding farewell to her plans to exercise some control over her future.

'Beyond that? You have nothing to worry about.

You have but to be as lovely as you are.' Portia patted her hand.

'It will be fine,' Cassie said, to steady a sudden rush of nerves.

'Better than fine,' Portia assured her. 'It is only a dance, and you are more than skilled in the popular steps. If at any time it becomes too much? Fan yourself and ask the nearest gentleman to fetch you a lemonade. It will pass the time and spare your toes from being trod upon.' Her advice finished; she led Cassie to stand by the velvet rope that separated the dance floor from the rest of the room.

It was only a few moments before Lady Jersey arrived at her side to introduce her to her first partner, Mr Gerald Balard.

Mr Balard was pleasant enough, though he laughed too loudly and talked too quickly. But he was a fair dancer and led her through the Scottish reel with no trouble. As they stood out at the bottom of the set, she pretended to listen as he chattered about a carriage horse he'd purchased, a little relieved that he showed no signs of caring to know more of her.

Perhaps Portia had been right. Her job this evening was to look pretty and dance. If all the gentlemen were like Mr Balard, her intellect would not be required. So she kept smiling, scanning the crowd for familiar faces.

It was then that she noticed the Duke of Westbridge, watching her intently from the side of the room.

She looked away quickly, for she did not want to seem too interested in someone with whom she should be barely acquainted. Especially not the most notorious man in the room. Beside her, Gerald had gone on to describe the phaeton that the new horse would pull. She had no idea when the topic had changed, so she redoubled her smile and increased her nodding until the next part of the dance began and they had no time to talk.

When the song ended, her partner led her back to the side of the room where another man waited for his dance, and the game began again. The gentlemen chosen for her were all equally pleasant and ranked no higher than baron. She wondered if this indicated the maximum height she was to aspire to, given her deficiency of birth. Or perhaps, because it was the first ball of the Season, she was expected to prove herself worthy of more noble partners.

It did not really matter. A title was not an indicator of character. Westbridge was proof of that.

She stole another glance in his direction. He did

look fine in knee breeches, his cravat snowy white and his chapeau-bras tucked under his arm.

Appearances could be deceiving.

She turned away, concentrating on her latest partner, equally well dressed but devoid of charm.

As she was led to the side of the room for the fourth time, the man she'd been spying on appeared at her side, smiling expectantly at her last partner until he blanched under the scrutiny and walked away. Then, he looked down at her and smiled. 'Alone, at last.'

'We are not alone,' she said glancing at the crowded room around them, hoping to see the next man who would partner her. But the orchestra was tuning up for a waltz and no one was coming to save her.

The Duke seemed to sense her dismay and ignored it, smiling. 'When I am with you, no one else matters.'

She snapped her fan open and waved it vigorously in front of her, trying to cool the blush that must be rising in her cheeks. Perhaps now was the time to ask for lemonade. If she did so, he might go away.

Or perhaps she could allow herself some small interaction. He would likely disappoint her, as all the other men here had, and it would be that much easier to forget him. 'That is very flattering, Your Grace. Do you use it often, when trying to turn heads?'

He laughed. 'Actually, yes. But there are rare times when I mean it.'

She nodded. 'So, you are telling me that I am one of a small group. I suppose I should be honoured.' She stared out at the dancers, pretending that his presence did not matter to her. 'Assuming your last comment referred to me and not another.'

'Touché.' He stared out into the room as well, then said, 'I was indeed, referring to you. I can honestly say you are the only person that has mattered to me in a very long time.'

Her fan froze in mid flutter as she tried to think of an answer to this florid compliment. Then, she remembered that she did not mean to complicate her life by admitting to visiting his bedroom. She snapped the fan shut and let it dangle from her wrist. 'Three days, at least, Your Grace. That was when you met me, wasn't it? At my ball in the Argyle Rooms?'

Now he stared at her for a moment, then said, 'So you say.' He glanced towards the orchestra. 'They are tuning up for the waltz.'

'I suspect so,' she replied. Would she have to contend with his attentions for the whole of the dance? She wondered how long she would be able to stay ahead of him, for he was far more experienced with this verbal fencing than she was.

'You must dance it with me,' he said in a voice as smooth and sweet as honey.

'Must?' She gave him another sidelong look. 'That is quite impossible. I am not permitted to waltz.'

'Rules are made to be broken,' he said and took her hand, pulling her gently towards the opening in the velvet barrier.

She looked around her, trying to contain her panic. She could not waltz or she would offend the patronesses. By tomorrow, all of London would know of her lapse in propriety.

But neither could she fight against his lead without creating an embarrassing scene. Where were Portia and Julian? She needed a rescue.

'They are out on the dance floor already and have eyes only for each other,' he said, as if reading her thoughts.

'I will lose my vouchers,' she said in an urgent whisper.

'Not over something as small as this,' he said, swinging her easily into his arms.

'They will evict you as well,' she added.

'Nonsense.'

'They would not admit Wellington himself, and

he was just a few minutes late and wearing trousers instead of breeches.'

'That was Wellington. I am me.'

'He conquered Napoleon.'

'And I shall conquer Lady Jersey,' he replied, spinning her around until she was quite dizzy.

She wanted to laugh, but the situation was far too serious. As she turned, she cast a frantic look in the direction of the lady he'd mentioned, trying to relay the wordless message that she'd had no real say in the predicament she'd landed in. But judging by the frown she received in response her side of the story might not matter.

'You are an excellent dancer, despite your lack of attention to your partner,' Westbridge said, smiling as his hand tightened on her waist.

The sudden stop forced her to look up, into his eyes.

'Better,' he said, beaming at her. 'It crushes my fragile spirit to think you would rather look at others than at me, now that I finally have you in my arms.'

'You are the most conceited creature alive,' she said, unable to contain herself.

He laughed again. 'Yes, I am. But you knew that already, didn't you?'

'I beg your pardon?' she said, giving him what she hoped was a confused smile.

'When you were in my room with me, after the duel,' he said, smiling back. 'Surely, you must have noticed that I was selfish. But you did not seem to mind it.'

'I'm sorry?' Now she frowned. 'I do not understand.'

His smile faltered for a moment, though his step did not. 'No one can hear us. You do not have to pretend that you don't know me.'

Portia had warned her not to encourage this man and admitting that she'd been alone with him in his bedroom was probably just that. 'You are my brother's friend,' she said. 'I know you as that, of course. We have been introduced. But only just this week.'

He nodded and his smile turned cynical. 'So this is how it is to be. We were strangers until just this week, were we?'

She said nothing in response, just blinked at him and waited for him to speak, hoping that whatever was to come was not too revealing.

'Very well,' he said with an exasperated sigh. 'We were strangers until just a few days ago. So, it will mean nothing to you that I wish to apologize to a certain young lady for something that occurred on our last meeting. What happened was very pleasant, but I regret that it upset her and would gladly have traded the kiss for even one more minute in her company.'

It was the sort of romantic declaration that any girl would long to hear, especially in the glow of candle-light with a waltz playing in the background. She could feel herself melting, and the truth bubbling up from deep inside her ready to burst out. If she was not careful, she would announce that he could have all the time he wanted, but she would not trade the kiss for anything.

And again, she reminded herself of the character of the man who held her. He was a womanizer with no time for inexperienced women. He might think, because of her parentage, that she was less than pure. If so, this whole conversation was a lie meant to lure her into doing something foolish.

So she smiled at him and said, 'It is a very interesting story. I hope, for your sake, that you find her.'

He spun her again. And as the room turned about her, she saw Julian and Portia, looking by turns angry and shocked. The conversation on the ride home would be difficult, and possibly soon. By the look on her brother's face, he wanted to drag her from the room before she could even finish the dance.

The Duke caught her again, and turned with her

so they could no longer see him. 'You look worried, my dear. Is there a problem?'

'I think my brother means to stab you again,' she said, forcing herself to smile.

'If he does, will you nurse me back to health?' he said with a hopeful look.

'You would be better off calling a surgeon,' she said, refusing to be moved.

'When I spoke to your father the other night, he said that your medical knowledge was almost equal to your local doctor and that you helped with all manner of emergencies.'

She was not sure which surprised her more: the fact that he had spoken to her father, or that he had asked about her. 'The village we lived in was small and we learned to make do if help was not available. I can set bones, deliver babies and treat simple illnesses,' she said, then added, 'I can also help with birthing lambs and cattle.'

He laughed. The sound was unexpectedly genuine compared to the conversations she'd had with other partners. 'If I see a ewe in distress when I am walking in Piccadilly, I will summon you immediately. Now, tell me, what do you do when you are not helping others?'

'Do?'

'For pleasure,' he prompted. 'On the rare times

you are not being useful to someone else, how do you pass the time?'

When she did not immediately answer, he said, 'You are allowed some leisure, when at home, I hope.'

'Yes,' she said slowly. 'It is just that no one has asked me about it before.'

He laughed again. 'You came here full to the brim with polite conversation and have no room for the mundane. I already know all I need to about the weather, the music and the disappointing refreshments. Tell me about yourself.'

Before she could form a response, the song ended and he released her with a sigh. 'Your answer must wait until our next meeting, I fear. For now, let me show you how to deal with your critics.' Then, he offered her his arm and escorted her off the floor and past her outraged brother to the place where Lady Jersey waited, her expression stern.

Westbridge bowed deeply to her, then looked up at her with a boyish smile. 'I have broken a rule again, haven't I?'

'Several,' the patroness said, raising an eyebrow. 'There is a flask in your pocket. And you know there is to be no drinking here.'

'I thought it was no drunkenness,' he replied with a shrug. 'I assure you, I am quite sober.'

'But very indiscreet for waltzing with Miss Fisk, when she has not been given permission.'

'She did say so,' he admitted. 'But I gave her little choice in the matter.'

Lady Jersey turned to her and gave her a look that made her knees go weak. Then, she said, 'Do not let it happen again.'

'Of course not, Your Ladyship,' she replied with an obedient curtsy.

'And you.' She turned to Westbridge.

He gave her an astonishingly innocent look.

'If you were not so well-heeled, and with a title so old…' She gave a small shudder. 'And so very single? You would not get away with half the things you do.'

'I am aware of the fact,' he said, giving her a smile that could melt the stoniest of hearts.

'The least you could do, if you mean to hang about here, making trouble, is choose some unfortunate girl and make her your wife.'

If possible, his smile grew even brighter. 'I will take that under advisement.' Then, he turned to Cassie, took her hand and raised it to his lips. 'Miss Fisk, thank you for the dance. It was delightful. And now, *au revoir*.' Then, he turned and hurried to the door before her brother could catch him.

Chapter Six

The next morning, Sebastian settled in his favourite chair at White's, drinking his coffee, and plotting his next move. His visit to Almack's had been a blend of triumph and frustration. Cassie was still refusing to admit that she was the woman who had cared for him so tenderly a year ago. But after dancing with her, he was even more sure that it had been her.

For a vicar's daughter, she was a surprisingly good liar. Perhaps that was why they suited each other. Like called to like. As an experienced prevaricator, he could appreciate the iron control she had over face and body. She had not frowned or flinched. She did not blink too fast or too slowly. If he hadn't been holding her in his arms, he might never have noticed the slight pause in her breathing before she delivered a falsehood. It was the barest hesitation and would have been lost in the noise of the room if his hand had not been resting on her ribs.

He had known she was both talented and lovely. But he had never expected her to be devious. It excited him almost as much as the kiss had done. And then, there was the air of assurance she had when sparring with him on the dance floor. She might think her cool responses would put him off, but he found them more attractive than the lures of a determined flirt. There was something about the way she pretended not to care that made him want her all the more.

At least, he hoped she was pretending. He was not sure what he would do if he discovered that she truly did not love him. Likely something as foolish and self-destructive as he had done before he'd met her.

But he had no intention of giving up hope until he had managed to sort truth from fiction in regards to the events of a year ago. He'd assumed the enigma of Cassie the nurse would be solved once he'd found her. Cassandra Fisk was a puzzle in her own right, and one he would delight in unraveling.

In the year he'd searched for her, he'd sometimes worried that he might be disappointed by the woman he found. What would he do if she was not as he remembered? But their meetings recently had laid those fears to rest. She had a sharp wit and was not afraid to use it. On the surface, she seemed cool and sensible, but he was sure there was a rebel underneath. He was her opposite: the world might think him reckless but he longed for stability. Each of them would find what they needed in the other: challenge, stimulation and ultimately, completion of the most satisfying sort.

He was lost in a fantasy of their shared future when her brother took the chair beside him and signalled the waiter for a drink. Then he turned to glare in his direction. 'Good morning, Westbridge.' He sounded like a man spoiling for a fight.

He had come to the wrong place. Sebastian was full of love for his fellow man, especially one who might soon be an in-law. 'Hullo, Julian,' he replied with an oblivious smile.

'Did you enjoy your visit to Almack's?' the other man said, his frown deepening.

Sebastian took a sip of his coffee. 'More so than usual. The place is not a favourite. But last night, the company was more interesting than usual.'

'You danced with my sister.' The innocent statement sounded like an accusation.

'That is what one normally does at Almack's. It is an assembly room. They hold balls. You dance at them.'

'The girls there are not to waltz until given permission,' Septon said, still grim.

'Because of a silly rule created by the she-dragons

that run the place,' Sebastian replied. 'The patronesses have too much power and wield it unfairly. You have said so, often enough. And your sister is well past the legal age to decide for herself what dances she can do.'

'She said something similar when I questioned her about it last night,' Julian said, his anger changing to frustration.

'Well, good on her,' Sebastian replied, unable to hide his approval. 'We danced at your ball, as well, and you didn't feel a need to track me down and question me about it.'

His friend responded with a silence that hinted it was exactly what he had wished to do and had resisted the urge. Probably because it would make him look as foolish as he did now.

'I danced with her because it was the thing to do,' Sebastian finished, keeping his tone bland. He made a nebulous gesture with his free hand. 'Assembly rooms. Balls. As I said before. She was the guest of honour, for pity's sake. One is expected to pay one's respects.'

'As long as that was all it was,' Julian answered, still suspicious.

'We were never out of your sight.' *Not this week, at least.* 'Are you really so protective?' Sebastian allowed himself a small, incredulous laugh to cover the sin of omission.

'If I think it is warranted,' Julian said. 'You know as well as I do what scoundrels men can be.' Though he spoke in generalities, the look he gave Sebastian was very specific.

'She is in no danger from me,' he said. It was true, in a sense. His intentions were honourable, though he doubted Julian would see them as such.

'That is good to know.' Julian gave him one last warning look before settling back in his chair and taking a sip of tea.

Sebastian sipped his own drink as well, his mind racing. If this conversation was any indication, there was no point in asking permission to pay court to her. Refusal was guaranteed. But that did not mean he could not gain something from it. 'Out of curiosity, who are you hoping to match her with?' He stared out into the room as he spoke, to prove that the answer mattered little to him.

Julian's face relaxed into a smile. 'Someone better than she was aspiring to, I should think. A decent fortune. Some land. A minor title.'

Sebastian laughed again. 'Were you planning to attach a man to the list? Or is the estate sufficient?'

At this Julian looked exasperated. 'It is up to her to choose the man. I exist only to vet his circumstances.' He gave a half shrug. 'I suppose the people who raised her would like to have some say in it, just as a courtesy.'

'The Fisks,' he said, hoping he did not look as sour as his friend.

'The vicar and I are coming at the problem from different directions,' Julian said.

'You view this as a problem?' Sebastian said, irritated on Cassie's behalf.

'She is twenty-six and unmarried,' Julian said. 'It is well past time for a decision to be made.'

'By Cass…' He stopped himself. 'By Miss Fisk.'

Julian ignored his slip and continued. 'Mr Fisk is less interested in finances and more in character. I suspect he would settle for a clerk or a grocer, as long as the man was honest.'

'And you don't mind a little tarnish on the family name?' Sebastian said.

'On the contrary. Only the most honourable man will do. But I do not think a life of denial is necessary to purify the spirit.'

'You would rather see her marry rich?'

'Yes.'

'Someone with a title, as you said before.'

Julian nodded. 'If such a man could be interested. Her situation is not ideal.'

Sebastian scoffed. 'She is a lovely girl. The right

man will be willing to overlook a past she had no part in making.'

'But the right man is definitely not a rake,' Julian added, giving Sebastian another speculative look.

'Well, good luck to you all,' Sebastian said, hoping that his sarcasm was not too obvious.

Julian smiled back as if he'd not noticed it at all. 'Thank you for your well wishes. It is just the beginning of the Season. Far too early to make any decisions. But I suspect it will not be too long before she has an offer. She is really the sweetest girl.'

'So she seems,' he said. He had thought so when she had come to him last year. But now that she chose to deny him, he was not so sure. There was a tartness in her, like the undernotes in fine wine that intrigued the palate.

'And in just this week, there are two promising candidates,' Julian added, not noticing his friend's silence.

Competition.

'Respectable?' Sebastian asked.

'Very. Mr Andrew Rutland. The son of the Earl of Grisham.'

'Second son,' Sebastian reminded him, calling up what he knew of the fellow.

'A son, all the same,' Julian replied. 'An heir would be nice. But there are those who would look down on her because of her birth, even though I've made it quite clear that she is acknowledged by the family. Still, the connection to the title should be worth something.'

'You are very stuffy, now that you have decided to take your reputation seriously,' Sebastian said. 'I never thought I would hear you talking about match-making and social connections.'

'Life was easier when I did not have a wife and sister to look out for,' he said with a shrug. 'A year ago, I did not expect to care as much as I do.'

'Rutland is a bit of a prig,' Sebastian could not help remarking.

'A prig who danced with Cassandra twice, last night, after you left Almack's,' Julian said.

Damn.

'Twice?' he said, giving his friend a suspicious look. 'That was flirting with propriety as much as my waltz was.'

'Your infraction likely gave him the nerve to request a second dance from Lady Jersey. It was you who put her in a forgiving mood.'

Damn, again.

'And it is better him than the alternative,' Julian responded.

'Who would that be?'

'Someone like…us.'

The pause was significant. He had been about to say *you*, only to soften the remark at the last minute to include himself.

'You have reformed your character,' Sebastian reminded him.

'Because of Portia.'

'You were still a rogue when you married her,' Sebastian reminded him.

'I did so for the worst reasons,' he said with a thoughtful smile. 'I thought marriage would be a quick salve to my reputation and had no intention of remaining faithful.'

'But that was not the way it turned out,' Sebastian reminded him.

'I am most satisfied with the result,' Julian said, a little smugly. 'But that is not to say I was a worthy husband in those first weeks. I would not want to put Cassandra through the difficulties I forced on Portia.'

'Far better to yoke her to someone as boring as Rutland,' Sebastian said with a grimace.

'It is up to Cassie to decide whether he is too dull to make a good husband,' Septon said taking another sip. 'And he is far from the only choice. There is Tobias Blake, as well. He is reading for the church.'

'Another vicar?' This was even worse.

'Fisk thinks he would be a good choice for her.'

'I imagine he would,' Sebastian said, wincing.

'It is what she knows,' Julian added as if this explained everything. 'It would be a stable life. I could guarantee the man a living on my estate.'

'She could live just across the way from the great house,' Sebastian said, spreading his hands as if setting the scene. 'I see her in a modest little cottage, keeping house for her lord and master…'

'You make it sound like indentured servitude,' Julian snapped. 'The wife of a clergyman is hardly as bad as that.'

'Nor is it the life one would expect for the daughter of a duke,' Sebastian countered.

'Not the legitimate daughter, perhaps,' Julian said with a sigh. 'I want the best for her, of course.'

'Of course,' Sebastian said with a grimace.

'But I am not sure that it will be possible.' At this, he was surprised to see a touch of worry on his friend's face. 'Do I think she deserves to be mistress of a great house and the protection and wealth of a titled husband?' He paused for a moment, then gave an emphatic nod. 'Of course I do. She has a spirit as noble as any member of my family. More so, if I am honest. She was raised to be a better person than I was, by people who lived the lessons they taught her.'

'She is a vicar's daughter,' Sebastian admitted.

'That appears to be what the gentlemen of London think of her,' Julian said, obviously frustrated. 'I fear they think she is both too pious and too unchaste. As if that is even possible.'

'She is neither of those,' Sebastian blurted, before remembering that he should have no opinion.

Julian did not seem to notice, too wrapped up in his own problems. 'It is not as if I can command gentlemen of rank to court her.'

'I am sure there are many powerful men that will want her, if you give them the time to come forward,' Sebastian said. Then, before he could stop himself, he said, 'I…'

'*You*, should learn to get out of the way and give them the space to do so,' Julian said, his manner turning from confidant back to guardian.

'Because it's not as if I could be a candidate for her hand,' Sebastian said, remembering that he was supposed to be uninterested.

Julian nodded in approval. 'I am glad that you will admit to the fact. Now stop playing about and distracting her from her business.'

'Her business?'

'The business of finding a proper husband from whoever has the good sense to offer for her. The last thing I need is for her to take your flirting seriously.'

'I don't think you have to worry about that,' Sebastian said, thinking of the way she had responded to it so far. 'She is a very sensible girl.'

'And you are sensible as well, are you not?' Julian gave him another warning look. 'Because I do not want to have to explain this situation twice.' This last was said with a finality that reminded him of the day they'd met a year ago which had ended with him fainting from blood loss as a vicar murmured prayers over his body.

He smiled at Julian, as if they were in complete agreement, and turned his thoughts to the memory of the beautiful Cassie bending over him, whispering encouragement and stroking his cheek. 'Do not worry. I am sure, before the Season ends, she will have a man as devoted to her as she is to him.'

'I am sure you are right,' Julian said, smiling again.

Sebastian set his cup aside and stood. 'Now, if you will excuse me, I have business to attend to.'

Julian raised his cup in salute. 'Of course.'

'Send Portia my love. And to your sister?' He turned back and blew a kiss. Then he hurried out the door and into the street without waiting for a response.

Rutland and Blake.

The fact that there might be other men interested in her was not a surprise, but he had not expected them to arrive so soon. They were not the most impressive men in London and in his opinion, Cassie deserved far better.

Him, for instance.

There was no time to lose. The longer the Season went on, the more likely it was that other names would be added to the list of suitors. He needed to spike the guns of his rivals and spend all the time he could in the company of the beautiful Cassandra. And he must do so without her brother noticing the fact.

It would be tricky, of course. Shakespeare had said the course of true love would not run smooth. He had no experience in it, but the quote appeared accurate. He had also heard something about faint heart never winning fair lady. So he should best get about it, no matter how difficult it might be.

He signalled for his carriage and hopped in before it had fully stopped, ordering the driver to take him to the Septon townhouse. The first step would be to find the lady in question, and the best time to do that was when he knew her brother was not at home.

It was a beautiful day on Bond Street and Cassie was taking advantage of a short break in her busy social schedule to do some shopping. Julian was away from the house, as he often was during the day, and Portia had gone as well, visiting friends. Neither of them would object to her going out on her own, as long as she was accompanied by a maid.

At least, she assumed they would not. She had not actually asked anyone. And, when Portia had suggested they make social calls together, Cassie had hinted that she had a megrim and was not in the mood for visiting. When she saw her sister-in-law later in the day, she would tell her another fib about hoping fresh air and a walk would clear her head.

The air in London could hardly be called fresh, compared to the country. With that excuse, she'd have been smarter to have gone to Hyde Park. That was the trouble with lies. Even small ones were so hard to keep straight.

But she had been afraid that the truth would make her seem ungrateful. She had wanted to get away, if only for a little while. To be by herself with no one watching her every move and interaction so they might offer critiques once she was done. So she had convinced Bessie that they should walk to Bond Street, promising the maid an ice at Gunter's if she did not report every detail of the trip to the master of the house.

It was probably too much to hope that she would have any real privacy during her Season. To be offered up as a candidate for marriage to London's elites required that she behave as if she had never been out of sight of her guardians, nor wished to be so.

But it was rather ridiculous. She had been of age for five years and had wandered freely around the countryside with no fear for her reputation. She had never done anything wrong and the men around her, who were simple working people, had better manners than some of the supposed gentlemen she'd met in town.

Then, as if she needed an example to prove her point, the Duke of Westbridge appeared from around the next corner and walked down the pavement towards her.

She glanced around her, searching for escape. She did not want to cut him in public, but neither should she be talking to him. If someone noticed them and told her brother, she would come home to the same lecture she'd received after last night's waltz.

But this side of the street seemed lined with tobacconists and boot makers, the sorts of places a lady had no reason to frequent. There was nothing for it but to keep moving forward and hope that he passed her with no more than a tip of his hat and a polite hello.

It had been too much to ask. He walked towards her with purpose and a bright smile. 'Miss Fisk,' he said, reversing his direction to walk with her. 'So good to see you again. It has been so long.'

'It has been hours,' she corrected.

'It seems longer. May I escort you to your destination?'

'That will not be necessary,' she said, drawing a little closer to Bessie to remind him she was chaperoned. 'I have no fixed goal, but I am sure I do not need assistance finding my way.'

'All the more interesting,' he said. 'We shall ramble together.'

'I don't want to divert you from your shopping,' she said, trying to sound kind.

'I had no plan in coming here, but to find you,' he said and pretended to gaze into the window of the shop they were passing.

Their eyes met in the reflection on the glass. 'What do you mean by that?' she said, frowning.

'Simply that I stopped by your home and inquired after your location.'

'Who told you where I had gone?' she said, annoyed.

He smiled back at her from the glass. 'I did not bother with the front door as Septon's butler is notoriously enigmatic. I went straight to the back entrance and bribed a maid. She saw your maid speaking with a footman.' He turned and winked at Bessie who blushed furiously.

Cassie stared at him for a moment, unsure of how to respond. She had known he was wicked. But it appeared he was clever, as well. And more persistent than she'd expected him to be. A gentleman would have taken the hint and pretended to forget their past, just as she was doing. Did he think she would tumble into bed with him just as she had done last year?

The idea should not have made her want to smile. Despite the warnings from Julian and Portia that their friend had no redeeming qualities, some moonstruck part of her brain was flattered by his interest. Did she really think herself so alluring that he had any feelings for her than lust?

It was far more likely that he planned to blackmail her with last year's impropriety. Or perhaps he had not really forgiven Julian and meant to hurt her brother, through her. Now he was grinning at her, waiting to see how she responded to his intrusion.

'Well, you have found me. What do you mean to do about it?' She said and glanced around her at the people on the street. 'And before you answer, know that, if I call for help, there are dozens of gentlemen around us who will come to my aid.'

He blinked at her, surprised. 'Why should you

need any help? What must you think of me that you would say such a thing?'

'I only know of you by what I have heard from others,' she said. 'And that has all been bad.'

'Your brother, no doubt. I was speaking to him just this morning and he warned me of dire consequences should I keep pestering you.' He looked endearingly innocent. It was probably why he could get away with the things he did.

'Do you ignore everyone who tells you to go away?' she said.

'Most of them,' he admitted. 'It does not happen as often as you think.'

'And if I tell you to go away?' She held her breath, waiting for the answer.

'You have not actually done so,' he said, staring back at her.

It was a challenge. She should do as everyone suggested and send him away.

But what if he obeyed?

When she'd come to London, she'd assured her parents that she would not do anything foolish. To crave just a little more time with a man like the Duke of Westbridge was so unwise it bordered on stupidity. But she could not bring herself to say the words that might make him leave her. Instead, she sighed and turned away from the shop window to walk down the street in the direction she had been going.

He followed, falling into step at her side, and Bessie trailed behind them.

'You still have not answered my question,' she said without looking at him. 'Why did you come looking for me?'

'I wanted to continue our discussion of last night. Before our dance ended, I asked you what you did for pleasure. You did not have time to answer me.'

She hadn't. It had been such a novelty to find a man who wished her to talk about herself instead of just listening to him that she'd been too shocked to say a thing. It was even more shocking to find that he had remembered what he'd said and was still waiting for an answer. He was acting as if he really cared.

'I like to read,' she said. 'I paint and play the pianoforte.'

He was still staring at her expectantly.

'I am also skilled at needlework.'

He stopped.

So did she.

Bessie, who had not been paying attention, bumped into her, then took a step back.

Westbridge raised a doubtful eyebrow. 'I have come to suspect that, when girls make their come-out, their mothers empty their heads and replace their brains with a card file of appropriate conversation. You have used cards one through three on me now.'

'I am an ordinary girl, with an ordinary set of accomplishments,' she said, trying not to sound defensive.

He shook his head. 'Yesterday, you were telling me of birthing lambs. I expected to be similarly surprised when I asked your interests.'

'If I were to tell you how I passed the time in the country, you would think me boring at best, and simple at worst.' Even a consummate liar such as he would not be able to feign interest in the real her.

She turned away from him and began walking again at a somewhat quicker pace.

He hurried to catch up. 'Does it matter what I think of you? I did not think you had the need to impress me in any way.'

He was right. It shouldn't matter. Maybe, if he thought her dull, he would leave her alone. The thought made her sad in a way she did not fully understand.

'When the weather is fair and I have nothing more useful to do, I like to sit outside, under a tree,' she said. 'Sometimes I read. And sometimes, when the book is not interesting enough, I steal a bit of sugar from the kitchen and sprinkle it around an ant hill. Then, I watch the insects discover it and carry it inside to present to their queen.' She walked on, afraid to look in his direction.

When he did not say anything, she added. 'Sometimes, I take my sketchbook and draw pictures of them. Other insects, as well. My mother has declared my watercolours entirely inappropriate for display and requested I limit myself to flowers. But I refused.' When she glanced in his direction, he was grinning.

'A naturalist,' he exclaimed. 'That is much more the sort of thing I wanted to hear. Is it just ants that you fancy, or will any insect do?'

'I have a preference for ants. But bees are very interesting, as well. If none are to be found? Dragonflies, beetles…' She shrugged, embarrassed.

'You must tell me everything,' he said in an awed tone.

She shook her head. 'If you wish to learn about insects, I should think there are several clubs and societies here in London that could teach you far more than I.'

He skipped ahead of her for a moment and walked backwards in front of her. 'Certainly not, Miss Fisk. I do not want a dry scientific lecture on the subject.

I wish to hear your views. We must go somewhere quiet where you can tell me everything.'

'I do not think…'

'I know just the place,' he said, ignoring her protest. 'How do you fancy Scotland?'

She stopped dead again, sure that she could not have heard what she thought he'd said. 'What?'

'A pledge over the anvil,' he said, standing in front of her and patting his coat pockets. 'I have my mother's ring with me, and a pair of fast horses harnessed to a post-chaise. We could be out of London before you are missed and in Gretna Green in three days.'

It was the sort of wild, impetuous suggestion that she had dreamed of, but never expected to hear, especially not from the lips of the Duke of Westbridge. But dreams were all they were. Real proposals, the sort one got as a result of a London Season, were carefully orchestrated and all parties involved had agreed to the wisdom of the match.

And there was no wisdom to be found here. Her heart might be hammering out a yes, but that had more to do with the desire to run away from responsibility than it did with an urge to marry. In any case, the man in front of her was not to be taken seriously.

She responded the only way she could. She forced herself to laugh, surprised that it sounded almost natural.

There was a moment of silence. Then, he said, 'Have I said something amusing?' and looked at her with a raised eyebrow and a sardonic smile.

'I'm sorry,' she said, with an expression that was equally cynical. 'I assumed you had to be joking.'

His smile softened. 'What if I was not?'

Her heart was now beating so loudly she was sure he could hear it. She chose her words carefully, so he would not see how his suggestion had affected her. 'Then, I would assume that what you were offering was an attempt to get me away from my chaperones with the promise of marriage, only to abandon me after you got what you wanted.'

'What I wanted?' His words were low and seductive.

She sighed to steady her pulse and refused to succumb to them. 'Three days on the road is a long time for any girl to resist a practiced seducer.'

He smiled. 'Practiced seducer. I rather like the sound of that. And I have put quite a bit of time into honing my skills on that front.' He gave her another speculative look that made her insides flutter.

She took another steadying breath. 'It was not meant as a compliment.'

'I will take it as I see it,' he said, unbothered. 'You

are not interested in testing your assessment of me at an inn somewhere on the road?'

'Certainly not.'

'Not even if I promise to let you lock the bedroom door.'

'You have not said which side of it you would be on,' she reminded him.

Now he laughed. 'Point to you. Very well. I cannot persuade you to travel to Gretna Green.'

To emphasize her refusal, she stepped around him and began walking again.

He turned and hurried to catch up. 'Would a more conventional marriage interest you? I could get a special license. We might be wed in a few days' time with your friends and family in attendance.'

She resisted the urge to put her hands over her ears, afraid that it would be even more scandalous than the scene they probably presented. 'The world would likely think you had dishonoured me and were forced at sword's point to make the offer.'

'Not the whole world,' he replied. 'I do not flatter myself to think I am that well-known.'

'I am sure there are a few tribes in the Amazon who would not remark on our sudden vows. But anyone in London would gossip.'

He hurried in front of her and stopped, blocking

her way. 'Very well, then. A formal proposal. Banns read from the pulpit in St George's and the most elaborate ceremony possible, with an archbishop presiding.'

He meant to abandon her at the altar. Or humiliate her by cheating, once they were married. Either would hurt Julian as much as it did her.

He glanced down at the pavement between them. 'I will kneel here if you wish me to.'

'Have you gone mad?' she whispered, turning away to look in the nearest window.

'You would prefer that I wait until we are somewhere less public?' he whispered back, his head dipped close to hers so she could feel his breath against her ear.

She stepped away and stared up at him. 'I would prefer that you refrain from talking nonsense.'

'You find an offer of marriage from a peer nonsensical.' He stepped back as well, and for a moment, she wondered if she had actually offended him. The playfulness had gone from his tone and his posture was rigid.

What could she say that would make him stop teasing her? She knew every word was a lie. And yet, this bantering was utter and delicious madness. It made her want to run to the carriage he had suggested and let him sweep her off to Scotland, casting her honour away like a bridal bouquet, to land where it would, somewhere on the way to the life of happiness she'd imagined.

But it was not real, and she should not treat it as such. She would not be a fool for him, no matter how much she wanted to be. She gave him a direct look, and said, 'I have no illusions about my past or my future. I am a natural child—a bastard,' she said with blunt finality. 'Even with my brother's acknowledgement, it will count against me when an offer is made.'

'From some, perhaps,' he said.

'But not from you?' she said. 'We have barely met.'

'So you keep saying,' he said, his eyes narrowing slightly.

She ignored the challenge and went on. 'I do not take you seriously because, given who I am and who you are, it is far more likely you would offer me a slip on the shoulder than a church wedding.'

'And have your brother call me out for dishonouring his sister?' he said.

'Some would see your current actions as a long-delayed revenge.'

The idea seemed to shock him, as if he had seriously never considered what seemed obvious to her. When he spoke, there was a strange quality to the words, as if he had thrown away all the glib good humour to reveal a different speaker hiding underneath. 'Is there nothing I can say to you that will make you believe me?'

'That you are seriously offering marriage?' She stared back at him, equally pensive. 'I cannot think of anything.'

They stood together in silence for a moment, and she could not help wishing that she had not spoken. But it had been necessary to be direct, to make him understand the way things were. Perhaps her nursing had given him the wrong impression. She did not want to be part of some game he was playing with Julian, nor was she the sort who could deny all expectations placed upon her and refuse the future her family wanted for her.

She was beginning to worry that she would have to refuse him another time, when his manner changed. Like a man donning a coat to protect against chilly weather, the seriousness she had seen was covered over with suave smiles and the relaxed posture of a man who did not care what anyone thought of him, much less some country girl he'd met on the street. 'Well then,' he said on an exhaled breath. 'If that is the way it is to be, I shall not bother you further.'

He turned away, and then back. 'Not today, at least. *Au revoir*, Miss Fisk.'

'Goodbye, Your Grace,' she said, as he walked away down the street.

Chapter Seven

As Sebastian walked away, it took all his strength not to turn back. What good would that do, other than to give him one final glimpse of her? He had been refused before and was well acquainted with the process. One licked one's wounds. Drank too much. Wrote a bit of maudlin poetry. Threw it in the fire. And found another woman.

But he had been so sure this time that there had been something more between them. She had devoted a week of her life to caring for him. She had loved him then in a way he did not understand. It was beyond the physical, two souls in communion. The only thing he could compare it to was the bond he'd had with his grandmother, who had loved him unconditionally.

But it was different than that.

Perhaps he did not know enough about love to find it for himself. But he suspected she did, and he had wanted her to teach him. About love, and perhaps about insects, as well.

He smiled. She had opened herself to him, just for a moment. If he wanted to win her, he needed to do the same.

He was not used to being vulnerable, especially not to a woman. But this one had already seen him at his weakest. Then, she'd shown him nothing but kindness. That, and a hint of the same dry wit she was showing him now. It was delightful, just as it had been a year ago. He wanted her now, just as he had then.

She might want him, but she did not believe in him. She did not trust him. Probably because he'd given her no reason to. He had been so eager to outpace her other suitors that he had charged ahead with his plans for their future and given no thought to what she might want from him or any other man. Seduction was a dance. But so was courtship and the steps were more elaborate and unfamiliar to him.

He must hope that he had not ruined it all by today's actions. If he could not have her love? Perhaps her friendship would be enough to sustain him. He would not even have that if she was convinced that his every action was an attempt to spite Septon or dishonour her.

A thought occurred to him and he darted into the

next shop he passed and scanned the glass cases for only a moment before signaling the shopkeeper and explaining what he needed, sketching a design on a scrap of paper the man produced.

What he wanted was simple, nothing more a token of apology. The man said that because of the unique nature of the piece and his desire for it to be finished quickly, it would be expensive. Sebastian assured him that the money did not matter. He could double the price if it could be done today.

The jeweler was hesitant. But it took only a moment for greed to win out over irritation, and he promised that the job would be ready by evening, and delivered to the Duke's townhouse, should that be convenient.

It was. Very much so. And it left Sebastian more than enough time to decide how best to present it, that he might wipe away the mess he had made of the morning. Then, perhaps she would allow him to begin again.

Later that evening, Cassie joined Julian and Portia at the dinner table, relieved to have a night without any planned activity. After what had happened on Bond Street, she did not think she could bear to go through the social niceties as if nothing momentous had happened.

'Did you have a restful day?' Portia asked as the soup was served.

'I took a nap, and then went shopping,' she replied, quickly adding, 'I took Bessie as a chaperone.' Then, she waited nervously for someone to announce that she had been spotted speaking with the forbidden Duke of Westbridge.

'Did you purchase anything interesting?' Portia said.

'I was browsing. Nothing more.' She took a spoonful of lobster bisque. 'The bookstore had several new titles.'

'I have an account there,' Julian said. 'Feel free to make use of it.'

The conversation turned to popular books with no further comment made about her leaving the house.

When dinner ended, they retired to the sitting room for an equally uneventful evening of patience and needlework. It acted as a balm to her frayed nerves and was one more proof that she had been right to refuse the Duke. She could not imagine him sitting comfortably for an evening in a room where nothing was happening. They were too different in temperament to make a good match.

Not that he had been serious. He was up to something, she was sure. He could not really mean to choose a wife based on one year-old kiss. There must be a hundred woman he knew that well. Why her?

And had she really told him that she fed ants? The fact that he'd proposed after that announcement was one more proof that he was only joking. Or perhaps it was an act of pity, for he must have thought her mad.

When they went upstairs to prepare for bed, she was still pondering over it. Why had she spoken of ants? Why not rabbits, or birds? Even hedgehogs would have been better.

Or moles.

She winced. Bessie, who had been combing her hair, stopped, assuming she'd tugged too hard.

'It is all right,' she replied, and glanced at the crystal vase that held a fresh lilac. 'Is that a new flower?'

'Yes, miss. It was delivered to the back door for you.' She grinned and tapped a folded piece of paper on the table. 'There is a note.'

She reached for it, trying not to seem too eager. The single word SORRY was written in elegant script in the centre.

She turned it over and raised it to the light to convince herself that there was no hidden message there, before turning to look at the flower. Something glittered amongst the purple blossoms of the cone. She pushed them out of the way with a fingertip to see the gift that had been wired to the stem.

It was a stick pin of the sort that one might see on a man's lapel or pushed through the linen of a cravat. She had seen women wear them on occasion, but they usually favoured larger, more dramatic jewels. The head of this one was so small it might go unnoticed when pinned on a spencer or pelisse.

It was a golden ant, the body made from bits of amber and the legs and antennae from fine gold wire. She untangled it from the flower and pressed a hand to her mouth to hide her smile.

It was the sort of gift that only a kindred spirit would know to give. When she wore it, he would know without her speaking that he had been forgiven. No matter what happened between them, she would cherish it.

She held it in her fist as Bessie tossed the nightgown over her head, and then carried it with her, setting it on the nightstand next to her as she climbed into bed and pulled the covers up to her chin. As she drifted off to sleep, her mind was filled with the golden glow of amber and the memory of a man's wicked smile.

The next day, Julian had promised a surprise that he assured her would be more to her tastes than some of the other events of the Season. 'Since you enjoyed your life in the country, I thought you might like to get out of the city for an evening,' he said as they shared a late luncheon. 'There is a tea garden that I have frequented you might find interesting.'

'Not Vauxhall,' she said, smiling. She had been there once before, and though it was very pleasant, it was quite busy and did not really feel like an escape from London.

'The Montpellier is far smaller than Vauxhall,' Portia said, smiling. 'But there are some nice greens for lawn bowling, and you may pet and feed the cows that provide the cream for the syllabubs.'

'Really?' Cassie stifled a smile. It was proof that Portia had spent too much time in the city if she thought petting a cow was a novelty. Still, it sounded like a delightful way to spend an evening. She hurried upstairs and changed into a sensible walking dress of tan muslin and added a green linen pelisse that would keep out the chill of an evening outdoors.

Before she left the room, she went back to the night table and retrieved the amber ant that she'd received from Westbridge, pinning it under a ruffle on her bodice. It was doubtful that the Duke would be in attendance, for the garden they would be visiting was in Walworth and quite out of the way. But it was the perfect bit of jewelry for a night of al fresco entertainment.

When she'd returned to the ground floor, Julian had summoned the carriage and helped her into it for the ride to the edge of the city. Their destination was even better than they'd described. A box had been reserved for them that was cut into one of the hedges that surrounded the garden. As they sat at their table, hornbeams surrounded them on three sides. The fourth was framed with gauze curtains, which were rustic in daylight but took on a magical air as the sun began to set.

Mr Rutland joined them a short time after they arrived, which Cassie suspected was part of the surprise they'd promised. In truth, she'd rather have petted the cows. Mr Rutland seemed very nice. Or perhaps it was that he did not seem too bad. She did not feel enough for him to care which of the two it was.

'Miss Fisk,' he said, bowing over her hand and smiling.

'Mr Rutland,' she replied, smiling politely.

'It would please me if you would call me Andrew.' He looked at her expectantly.

I imagine it would.

Since she could not think of a polite way to refuse

him, she continued to smile and said, 'Of course, Andrew. And you must call me Cassandra.'

He smiled and sat down beside her, helping himself to the light supper that had been laid for them, chatting amiably with Julian and casting occasional devoted looks in her direction. But she doubted he had any real interest in the content of her mind. When he bothered to speak with her, he limited their topics to the quality of the food and the superlative weather.

It made Cassie think of the card file that Westbridge had described, and the acceptable conversations that young ladies were allowed to have. Was that really all men wanted from the women they married?

She toyed with the pin on her lapel, wondering if Andrew would notice it. If he did, would he find it odd? Somehow, she doubted that he would have given such a thing to her. His courtship thus far had been lukewarm and very traditional. She suspected the ring she might be offered would be expensive but tasteful and made from diamonds as cold as ice.

After they'd dispensed with the bread and butter and were waiting for a plate of tea cakes, Andrew suggested a game of lawn bowling and went off with Julian for a while, leaving her alone with Portia.

Once the men were gone, her sister-in-law gave her an encouraging look. 'Well?'

'What?' she responded, pretending not to understand.

'Do you like him?'

She took a sip of her tea, which had gone cold, and refilled the cup from the pot.

'You are avoiding the question,' Portia said, disappointed.

'Yes, I am,' Cassie said. 'Because I do not know how to answer. I like him.' She took another sip and added a lump of sugar. 'But that is all.'

'You do not know him very well,' Portia said, pushing her cup towards the pot.

Cassie refilled it, as well. 'Three dances. And during them, I learned far more about him than he learned about me. Yet, he seems to like me very well.'

'It would be a good match,' Portia said thoughtfully.

'For him as well, I think,' Cassie said. 'He wishes to know Septon and to be part of his family.'

Portia sighed. 'I had hoped that there might be more.'

Cassie did not like being a disappointment, so she said, 'There still might be. It is too early to tell.'

Portia seemed encouraged by this and whispered.

'Perhaps, after this evening, you will like him better. You have not seen the surprise, as yet.'

'What might that be?'

'When he returns from bowling, he will offer to show you the gardens,' Portia said her eyes lighting with mischief.

'And you want me to go with him, unchaperoned?' Cassie responded. This was a surprise.

'There is a hedge maze,' she replied. 'It is very pretty at dusk.'

'Very dark, I suspect,' said Cassie, sipping her tea.

'There are torches. And it is not so large that you will be lost for long,' Portia said, as if she spoke from experience.

'Are you suggesting that I allow Mr Rutland to take liberties?'

'Not if you do not wish him to,' Portia replied. 'But a single kiss will do no harm, if you wish for one.'

Cassie was not sure that was true. The kiss she'd gotten from Westbridge had caused no end of trouble, so far. But she had enjoyed it. Perhaps, when the moment came, she might feel differently about Mr Rutland.

Andrew, she reminded herself.

'You can say no, if you wish,' Portia said, sensing her lack of enthusiasm.

'I can,' Cassie said. 'I think I will wait until the moment arrives to make my decision.' But from the relief she felt at the thought of refusing, things did not look promising for Andrew.

A short while later, the gentlemen arrived, bringing the cakes with them. And after a slice of sponge with raspberry jam, Andrew offered to show her the gardens.

When Cassie looked to Portia for support, she replied, 'We will follow in a little bit. I think I would like another piece of cake.'

It was probably just as well. She would need to make a decision about Andrew Rutland sooner or later. Tonight was as good a time as any. So when he rose, she took his hand and let him lead her out of the box and down a crushed stone path towards the maze.

'It is a lovely night,' Andrew said.

Cassie was tempted to tell him that they had covered this conversational ground before. Instead, she forced herself to do what was expected of her and replied, 'Yes. Lovely.'

'The gardens are lovely as well,' he added. 'Not so lovely as the ones on my father's estate. Those are much larger. But not open to the public, of course.'

'Of course not,' she said. Did he covet those grounds, she wondered? He was not the heir to them.

They would not come to him, unless both his father and older brother died. Nor had he done anything to create or care for them.

It was strange to brag about a thing that one was adjacent to but had no part in. Unless one had no real accomplishments of one's own, other than a family name and prospects of success if one married well.

'We have more roses. But we do not have a hedge maze,' he said, unaware of her doubts. He gestured to the topiary arch that was before them. 'Would you like to venture in?'

When she hesitated, he said, 'You need not be afraid. I am here to protect you.'

This was nothing more than a clever arrangement of shrubs. Only a complete ninny would be frightened by it. Perhaps that was what he thought she was. But it was not really the planting she was worried about. She wanted to see that. Just not with him.

'I have never seen a maze before,' she admitted, glancing around her at the other couples wandering around the gardens. The worst that might happen was a stolen kiss. She would survive it and be back with Julian and Portia in a few minutes.

'Come along, then,' he said, pulling her gently forward through the entrance. 'You will find it very pleasant.'

He was not exactly wrong. She did like the maze.

It was very green, and very dark. She inhaled the rich, live smell of the walls that surrounded them and immediately felt calmer. There was something so peaceful about being out in nature, feeling the chill in the air as the sun set, and bathing in the silver moonlight.

But she could not help thinking it would be better to be walking with someone else. Or to be alone, walking barefoot in the grass. That was a rather wicked thought. She could imagine herself in just a shift, or even less, focused on the night sounds and the touch of the breeze.

'See?' he said. 'It is nice, here.' Her hand was tucked in the crook of his arm, and he held it close to his body. He was probably trying to keep her warm, but the grip was uncomfortably tight.

They walked forward a short distance and turned left, then right, then left again. There was another straight length that she suspected ran along an outside wall, then another turn with a bench at the corner where a couple sat, kissing. Beside her, Mr Rutland chuckled, but led her past without further comment.

'Are we nearing the centre?' she asked. By her estimation, they must be. But she was quite turned around and not sure she could find her way out again.

He shook his head and led her down a blind alley and past another amorous couple, then back again to turn in the opposite direction. 'I know a spot where we will be able to see the moon. It is full tonight.'

She gave him a sidelong look. He walked and spoke as if he knew exactly where they were going. But if that was true, why had they taken the false turning a moment ago? The only reason she could come up with was that he wanted her to be disoriented and dependent on his guidance.

It was probably supposed to be romantic. But she did not like the feeling of being at a disadvantage. Nor did she like being lied to. Now she was pretty sure that they were going back the way they had come, but she might be confused. This was the dead end they'd been down before, and there was no reason to go this way. But by the time she thought to question him, they were alone and facing a wall of hornbeam.

'There,' he said as if they had reached a destination. 'The moon is just above us.'

She looked up. He was correct. She could have seen the same thing from the table, while having tea. But then, they would not have been alone, and he could not have placed his fingers on the tip of her chin so he could kiss her as she was looking up.

The kiss was short and quick. And it would have

been much sweeter if she had been eagerly waiting for it. Instead, it was a thing expected but not longed for. That made her a little sad.

He seemed content with it, though. He was smiling down at her. 'You are very beautiful in the moonlight.'

'Thank you.' Was she supposed to thank him? She swallowed nervously. When he did not reply, 'We should be heading back. This is obviously not the way to the centre.'

'How unfortunate for us,' he said, wrapping his arms around her to pull her close. 'I fear we are quite lost.'

'Not for long,' she said, trying to step back. 'We have but to retrace our steps and we will be right again in no time.'

'Or we could simply remain here awhile,' he said, pulling her close again. 'It is not often that we get an opportunity to be alone like this.'

It would not happen again, that was for certain. He probably thought he was being playful. In response, she should be feeling a thrill of excitement and not a sense of dread. Maybe because she had given him a gentle hint that she was not interested, and he had ignored it. Perhaps she needed to be clearer. 'I think we should find the others,' she said in a firm tone, looking back down the path towards escape.

'Not until you pay a forfeit,' he said.

'That is not the sort of game I came here to play, Mr Rutland. Now, if you will excuse me, I wish to go back to my family.'

'Andrew, please,' he said, ignoring the rest of her words.

She stepped out of his arms again. But as she tried to push past him, he grabbed her hand, spinning her around to face him. 'We will leave in a minute, no more than that.'

'Now,' she repeated, trying to pull away. But his grip was surprisingly firm. On the dance floor, he had been very gentle and his manners had been perfect. But here, alone and in the dark, he was very different. Another kiss seemed inevitable.

She closed her eyes, not because of any romantic foolishness, but to pray that no one saw them. If they were seen, she would be forced to accept a proposal, or disgrace. As his mouth covered hers, she decided that she would rather choose public ruin than to let this go on much longer. She could never marry a man who treated her this way when they were alone, no matter how polite he might be in public.

His lips were moving over hers, his tongue licking against her tightly pursed lips. It made her want to shudder. She could remember the kiss she'd shared while tussling on the bed with Westbridge, and awkward and shocking as it had been, it was infinitely preferable to what was happening now. Though she'd tried to tell herself afterwards that he had forced her, he had not held her as tightly as Andrew Rutland was. He had not demanded she submit or ignored her refusal. That kiss had been over too quickly. But this one seemed to go on and on.

She thought of the couples they had passed, too busy in their own lovemaking to answer a cry for help. How long would it take for Julian to miss her? And what would happen in the meantime?

Chapter Eight

After their meeting on Bond Street, Sebastian had promised himself that he would not trouble Septon's sister again. Yet, here he was, lurking in the bushes like a footpad, hoping to catch her alone.

He made sure he was not being observed and reached into his coat pocket for his flask, taking a long drink to numb the feeling of embarrassment. The last year had been frustrating. But through it all, he'd carried a sense of hope. He would find the woman who loved him, tell her he returned her feelings and all would be fine. But loving a dream was easier than the reality of Cassandra Fisk.

If he turned the clock back a day and a half to the moment before she had refused his offers of marriage he could at least go on flirting with her and assuming that she would admit to their first meeting. Once she trusted him enough to do so, he could propose and she would accept.

At a minimum, he could have written a better apology than the one word he'd sent her. He'd thought himself quite clever giving her a flower, a pin and an unsigned note. When he saw her again, in a few days, or perhaps a week, he'd planned to be cool and composed and as mysterious as she was. He would know by her reaction if he had ruined his chances or was open to another advance.

As a gentleman, he would abide by the consequences, either way.

That had been his plan yesterday. But he'd spent the night thinking of all the other men who would be courting her in the meantime. She was a desirable woman and he was not the only one who had noticed the fact. He could not afford to make mistakes as he had yesterday. In a week, she could be married to someone else, and he could be nothing more than a distant memory to her.

This morning, he'd found himself back at the servant's entrance of the Septon townhouse, bribing the kitchen maid to discover the family's evening plans so he could follow her and see who she was with and what they were doing.

When and if he settled the matter of Cassandra's future, he would have to speak with Julian about his talkative staff. For the most part, the servants in the Septon house were loyal. But little Meg in the kitchen had an invalid mother and a brother with weak lungs. It had not been hard to gain her loyalty, in exchange for enough money to give security to her family. Septon might want to sack her for the indiscretion, but Sebastian would gladly have her in his house for the service she'd provided.

Today, she'd told him that the carriage was being readied for a trip to the Montpellier Tea Garden. The place was quaint, though he usually preferred more substantial entertainments. But it was not as if one could take a vicar's daughter to a gaming hell. If he meant to marry Cassie, he'd best get used to milk cows and tea biscuits.

Or, perhaps not. Septon was not about to invite him along on tonight's outing, and the clientele at the place was usually working class with only a smattering of the upper crust. It would be hard to explain his presence, should he be noticed. He should stay away, since he had promised Julian that he would not get in the way of Cassandra's happiness.

He'd promised himself the same thing yesterday. She needed time to follow her heart. But what if that traitorous organ was leading her away from him? If he had stayed at home tonight, he would have been tortured by the idea that she was strolling through a moonlit garden with someone else. So, instead of keeping a shred of pride, he was wandering in Montpellier alone, sticking to the shadows and hoping to catch a glimpse of her and whoever she was with.

He knew from experience what would happen if the *ton* learned that he was trailing after a country virgin like Caro Lamb stalking Byron. He would be lucky to be viewed as a laughingstock.

More likely, people would think him pathetic, just as they had when he'd come into the title. He'd been such an awkward young man. Lonely, as well. Grieving a father who had been both a mentor and friend. He'd had the daft idea that a hasty marriage would fill the void in his life. And to have chosen Francesca as the object of his love…

He stole another drink from the flask. He'd vowed that he would never again play the fool for a woman. He had kept that promise for nearly seven years. But apparently there was no changing his true character. Time and experience had not changed the fact that he was a mooncalf.

As if to prove it, he caught sight of Cassie walking towards him, deep in conversation with the gentleman who escorted her.

Rutland. The man he least wanted to see. The fellow was Julian's choice for brother-in-law, young, handsome and of good family. He was also leading Cassie to the perfect place for a romantic proposal. Only an idiot would choose a street corner on a busy day when there were secluded benches on a moonlit path.

Suddenly, his heart was racing and his mouth dry. Rather than standing his ground and greeting them as if nothing was wrong, he stepped behind a boxwood topiary trimmed in the shape of a squirrel.

They passed close enough so he could hear Rutland going on about his father's roses.

Did Cassie like roses? Did she prefer them to lilacs? Dammit to hell, he had rose gardens and hothouses of his own on his estate. He could fill her bedroom with them, if that was what she wanted. Instead, he was hiding behind a big green rodent while another man stole his one true love.

He ran a hand over his brow, covering his eyes. He should go home. If he had misunderstood the situation and she wished for another man, he should not stand in the way. What was his love worth if he forced it on an unwilling recipient?

But he could not leave, yet. He had to hear for himself that she was marrying another. Then, perhaps, he could have some peace. He waited until he was sure that they had gone into the maze and rounded a corner or two before setting out after them. At each turn, he paused, listening for the sound of conversation. The drone of the tiresome

Rutland would carry through the leaves, even if he whispered.

He was more than a little familiar with the maze, just as he knew the dark walks of Vauxhall well enough to navigate them with his eyes closed. He had taken women to both of them on more than one occasion. There was a place a little way forward and to the left where the path turned back on itself ending in a blank wall of shrubbery with a nice view of the rising moon. It was just the place he'd have taken her, had it been him.

He followed the path around several bends, pausing before the last turn and leaning against the hornbeams to listen. What he heard was even more disappointing than an offer of marriage. It was the faint sound of lovers in an embrace. The silence broken with soft sighs and the rustling of clothing, barely louder than the whisper of wind in the leaves.

He froze in place and closed his eyes, wishing he had never come. The noises were like a knife to the heart. He needed to leave immediately, before they heard him lurking just out of sight. He pulled away from the hedge, careful to cause no creak of branches to alert them.

Then, before he could take a step he heard Cassie's voice, breathless, but firm. 'No.'

Rutland laughed.

Her next sound of protest was cut short as her mouth was covered with his.

Sebastian was around the corner before he had formed a plan. His first instinct was a primal desire to tear the other man apart. He was already upon them before he remembered that if they came to blows, he would certainly lose. Rutland was three inches taller and two stone heavier than him. Nor would it be wise to issue a challenge. He was a poor shot and a worse swordsman. He'd lost the only duel he'd fought.

But that did not mean he was without weapons.

He did not break stride but continued until he was standing beside the couple and could not be ignored. 'Rutland,' he said in a jovial tone guaranteed to annoy.

Rutland started and jumped away from his quarry, leaving her panting and blinking in the moonlight.

'And Miss Fisk, as well,' Sebastian said, smiling as if this was no different than a ballroom meeting. 'What a surprise to find you here.'

'Go away, Westbridge,' Rutland said in a warning tone. 'You are not welcome here.'

Not welcome to him, perhaps. But by the desperate look in Cassie's eyes, he was exactly where he needed to be.

He stared at Rutland and pulled the weight of generations of breeding around him like a cloak, remembering that, while Rutland might be a tower of muscle, he was merely a second son. As such, he was dust beneath Sebastian's boots. 'I believe the correct term of address is "Your Grace",' he drawled still smiling. 'We are not on informal terms, are we?' He let the last words drip with condescension, a reminder that they were not friends and never would be.

Rutland flushed at the insult, then tried to shake it off. 'You seriously want to argue about this now?' Did he think Sebastian might show mercy, and spare him from looking weak in front of a woman he was trying to impress?

'While the matter is fresh in my mind, yes, I think I do,' Sebastian replied, enjoying the moment. 'I should hate for this to become a difficulty between us. But I must insist that you apologize.' He dropped his smile and allowed his true feelings through. The annoyance. The disgust. The desire to pound Rutland with fists and title until nothing remained of him.

His manner changed as he turned back to Cassie. 'I might let it pass if we were alone. But Miss Fisk has witnessed your knavish treatment of me.' He shook his head as if amazed. 'The man does not recognize my rank. He speaks to me as if we are equals. Outrageous!' He gave Cassie a significant look.

It took a second before she recognized her cue to speak. Then she said, 'Indeed, Your Grace,' in a dutiful voice. But he noticed she was leaning back into the hedge behind her as if she needed its springy branches to hold her upright.

'Now, see here,' Rutland said looking around as if he feared that someone might see him being less than gallant.

'See here, Your Grace,' Sebastian prompted, puffing out his chest to display his injured dignity. He felt ridiculous, but it worked.

'Your Grace,' the man said in a whispered surrender. He seemed to shrink before he spoke again. 'It is a delightful evening. Let us not ruin it with an argument.'

'Of course not, old fellow,' Sebastian said, giving the other man a clap on the back that nearly sent him to his knees. 'Now that the matter is settled, you had best run along and find the centre of the maze. It defeats the point of the thing to hang about in a corner like this.'

Rutland looked confused for a moment, as if he was not quite sure how he'd come to being dismissed from a liaison that he'd arranged. Then he held out his arm to Cassie, ready to escort her.

'Ah.' Sebastian held up a finger of warning. 'I think Miss Fisk might need help finding the exit again. The poor girl looks quite pale. Perhaps she has taken a chill.' He turned to Cassie. 'Which would you prefer—onward with Rutland, or a return to start?'

'I have had enough fun for the evening,' she said inching closer to him. 'Perhaps we could go and find my brother.'

'Very well,' Sebastian said and made a shooing gesture to Rutland. 'Run along, then. Don't let us keep you.'

With a final, frustrated grimace, Rutland turned on his heel and walked back down the pathway, disappearing around a turn in the hedge.

As Andrew walked away, Cassie released her held breath and stared after him afraid to turn to her rescuer. What must he think of her? After the incident in his bedroom and now this, she must look like the sort of girl who gave kisses freely to anyone who asked. If the news of tonight's encounter was spread around London, her reputation would not survive. That such ruin would force her into marriage with Rutland made it all the more painful.

She turned back to Westbridge, unsure of what to say.

He stared back at her, his expression softening. 'You needn't worry. All I will say, should anyone ask was that Miss Fisk arrived on the scene and found us arguing. She could not possibly have been here earlier, for she is a virtuous young lady not prone to wandering in secluded spots with men.'

Was he teasing her? He was looking at her with the same bland expression he had used when harassing Andrew, as if he truly believed nothing had been going on. But it had been so much worse than that. She was so relieved and so grateful and had been so frightened. And now it was over. How would she ever thank him?

Without a word, she threw her arms around him, hoping he could understand.

For a moment, he seemed confused, barely responding to her assault. Then, his arms came up to hold her, gingerly at first and then in a gentle, brotherly way that was totally unlike the passion he'd shown in his bedroom a year ago.

'Did he hurt you?' He said it softly, into her ear, in a tone that was quite different than the playful one he had used only moments before. He sounded hard, resolved and dangerous.

She shook her head, still unable to express what she was feeling. Andrew hadn't done anything so very bad. But there had been the feeling when they were alone that he had wanted to. And that he was quite willing to take advantage of a situation to do anything he wanted, to her or anyone else.

'You are trembling.' He held her tighter, one hand sliding up to cup the back of her neck. 'Do not worry. You will get no trouble from me. You are perfectly safe.'

'I know,' she whispered and took a breath struggling to regain control of herself. 'How will I face him again? What shall I say to Julian and Portia?'

'You will not see him again.' He said in that firm, quiet voice that cut through the last of the panic in her head. 'And as for your brother?' She felt him shrug. 'Reality is what you say it is. You do not have to tell him anything, if you do not wish to.'

'But do not tell him that I have been holding you, please.' He laughed softly and she felt the expelled breath ruffle her hair. 'Tonight, you can trust me. Not all the time, perhaps. But in this moment, I mean to be a gentleman.'

His hands dropped away, and she was relieved to find she could stand without help. He offered her his arm, tucking one of her hands into his elbow much more gently than Andrew had done and giving it a reassuring pat. Then he walked her to the turning of the path and unerringly back towards the entrance of the maze. By the time they had gone a few feet, she was completely herself again and managed a smile.

'Very good,' he said softly. 'That's the spirit. You are fine. Everything is going to be all right.'

'But what if he talks?' she whispered hardly turning her head.

'Then he will be thoroughly sorry for doing so,' he said in a voice still pleasant, but with that undertone that raised the hairs on the back of her neck.

'Don't do anything rash on my account,' she said.

'Better me than Julian,' he replied, still smiling. 'Until he is sure of an heir, he shouldn't be taking any risks. Got to protect the title, after all. I suspect you and Portia would miss him, as well.'

'Don't talk rot,' she said, wishing she had a fan to flutter as a distraction.

He laughed and ignored her. 'He has too much to lose. But I?' She felt him shrug. 'I am quite unencumbered. No one would miss me in the slightest.'

That is not true.

She bit back the response. She should not be encouraging him. There was no real future in it. 'You know very well you are a duke, just as Julian is. But I suppose you are fishing for a denial.'

He laughed again. 'Unsuccessfully, it would appear. Never mind then. Just know that you needn't worry about any revelations. I will not speak and

Rutland would be far too embarrassed to.' He glanced down at her with what looked like genuine fondness. 'Now, keep smiling. I see Julian up ahead. Remember, we have been out for a pleasant stroll through the hedge maze, nothing more than that.'

She nodded nervously and did as he said, giving a forced laugh as they stepped clear of the bushes. She must have been gone longer than was proper for Julian was just ahead walking towards the maze at a purposeful pace. He looked angry, but his scowl deepened as he realized who she was with.

'Westbridge,' he said, his attention focused on his friend.

'Julian,' her companion replied, as sunny as ever.

'I see you are with Cassandra. Again.'

He shrugged. 'She lost her way. I was only bringing her back to the bosom of her loving family.'

'She does not need your help,' her brother said. He seemed to grow bigger as she looked at him, as if he was likely to explode at any minute. She needed to do something to calm the situation before he did.

'On the contrary,' she said in the firmest voice she could manage. 'I was in dire straits. I had no idea where to turn before His Grace arrived.' She added a pleading look that she hoped would convince her brother not to make a scene.

'What happened to Rutland?' he snapped. 'He was supposed to be watching you.'

'He had to leave,' Westbridge said, looking directly into Julian's eyes, and spoke with the same dire voice he'd used on Andrew.

Julian paused. His brow knit in confusion and he looked from the Duke to her and back again, as if trying to form the story of the last few minutes out of those few words.

Westbridge took advantage of the situation to escape. 'And now that I have done what I set out to do?' He gently disentangled her arm from his, raising her hand briefly as if to kiss it. Then he thought the better of the gesture and stopped it several feet from his lips, bowing his head in a kind of salute. 'I must take my leave.'

'Do that,' Julian said, back in control and staring at him until he turned and walked away.

Then, he turned to her. 'I thought I told you to stay away from Westbridge.'

'You also allowed me to be alone with Andrew Rutland,' she said giving him a rebellious look. 'You must pardon me if I take future advice from you with more than a few grains of salt.'

He looked shocked and reached out to take her hand. 'Did something happen?'

She was surprised to find her earlier fear replaced with anger. 'What would you do if it had?' she snapped. 'Force him to marry me? Do you not understand that at the same time you would be forcing *me* to marry *him*? You are practically forcing me now.'

'Cassandra,' he said, shocked. 'I did not mean to impose my will on you in any way.'

'You do not mean?' With a growl of frustration, she turned and walked away from him, back towards the table and Portia.

He hurried to catch up. 'Cassandra, you are acting like a child.'

She stopped to turn on him. 'You are treating me as a child, so you should not be surprised. I am twenty-six years old, Julian. I was happily on the shelf until you took it into your head to matchmake for me.'

'I thought… It is my job, Cassandra. As the head of your family, I should see you married.' The look he gave her was so confused that her anger evaporated, replaced by a desire to soothe him.

And that was a gift from her other family, she supposed. This tendency to mediate, even at the expense of her own happiness. 'I understand that you are trying to help,' she said. 'But I also have years of experience fending off unwanted advances of less than gentlemanly men.' It could not be proved by this evening's escapade. She had let herself to be lured into the darkness by a cad. That problem existed because she had followed the advice of her family instead of her own instincts. But blaming Julian for her troubles would not make them any better.

She sighed and said, 'You must trust that I will not do anything to put myself or my reputation at risk.'

He was still staring at her, doubtful.

'As for the Duke of Westbridge?' She took another breath. 'I will not allow my head to be turned by any of his nonsense.'

This seemed to satisfy him and he took her back to the table where a plate of sweets awaited along with tiny glasses of orgeat. As they enjoyed them, Julian and Portia exchanged significant glances, but neither of them said anything about the absence of Andrew Rutland. Nor did they comment when Cassie took his portion of the *gimblettes* and drank his cordial.

Chapter Nine

After parting from Cassie, Sebastian left the tea garden in a better mood than when he'd arrived. She had forgiven him. There was no doubt of it. She had not just let him hold her; she'd practically leapt into his arms.

And for a change, he had not ruined the moment. He'd held her gently, as if she was a baby bird that might be crushed by a wrong move. He had not kissed her, though he'd very much wanted to. Instead, he had set aside his wants and tended to hers, sure that he was trading one kiss today for the hundred kisses she would give him in the future to reward him for waiting.

Best of all, he'd felt something poking against him as she'd cuddled close. When he'd looked down, he'd seen the pin he'd given her, resting close to her heart. And she'd worn it when she hadn't expected to see him. It had to be a sign of her true feelings.

He must find a way to get her to reveal them.

But first he had other business to attend to.

He drove his carriage to a gaming hell in the East End, the sort of establishment few sensible gentlemen frequented. It was a good thing he had little sense, for it was just the place he needed to be tonight.

He tossed a coin to the doorman, to be sure his curricle would be there when he returned, and went in to find the proprietor, Miss Sally Green.

'Westbridge,' she said, opening her arms to greet him. 'It has been so long.'

'Because I wanted to hang on to the contents of my purse, you old cheat,' he said, giving her a kiss on the cheek. She was as he remembered her from the darkest days of his life, a motherly figure with grey hair piled high, and a gown of red silk. The jewels at her throat should have been a sign to him that the money he wagered was not going to leave the house.

Judging by the full tables around him tonight, London never lacked for green boys with more money than sense.

'What do you fancy, this evening?' she said, waving an arm. 'Faro? Dice? Something wicked?' She leered.

'Information,' he said. 'Nothing more.' He gave her his usual innocent smile.

'How flattering,' she said. 'But what do I know that a member of the House of Lords does not?'

'So much,' he said, 'So very much. You were a wealth of knowledge when I first came to town. On my first visit here, you could have fleeced me of everything I had that wasn't entailed. But you took just enough of my blunt to teach me a lesson.' He gestured to one of the few empty tables.

She sat down with him, signalling to a servant to bring them wine. 'You were a brokenhearted boy, thinking he could hurt the world by punishing himself.'

'I was an idiot,' he said, accepting the glass set before him.

'Love makes fools of us all,' she said taking a sip from her own. 'Now tell me, what do you want to know?'

'I need just a sliver of your knowledge as it relates to a single man,' he said, smiling in anticipation. 'Tell me everything you know about Andrew Rutland.'

The next day, when Cassie woke, she took the ant pin from its place on the night table and held it in her hand for a moment before getting out of bed. She stared down into the amber for a moment, stroking the beads with her finger. She had heard that sometimes insects were trapped in this stone. Perhaps it trapped memories, as well.

If so, this little ant contained the best and worst of what had happened on the previous night. The thought made her smile. Last year, she had rescued Westbridge. This year, he had rescued her. There was a lovely circularity to it, and an excellent end to their association.

She frowned. She had told Julian last night that he needn't meddle and that she knew right from wrong and men who were good for her from men who were not. But a part of her did not want this strange acquaintance to end. He was quite obviously wicked. Why else would he propose to her on a street corner?

She was far from fluent in philosophy, but her father had taken the time to explain Occam's Razor. The simplest answer, that Westbridge really wanted to marry her, was the most logical one. But she suspected the Duke had been taught the same lesson and was using the rule to trick her. He was up to something, and she had to be on her guard around him.

But whatever he was plotting, he had set it aside

last night, when she needed his help. She wanted to see him again, if only to thank him.

She rose and dressed, and at the last minute pinned the ant inside of her sleeve, where it could be close to her and unnoticed by others. It felt right to have a secret, a little bit of her old self to carry with her as she swanned about London acting like some kind of second-rate heiress. Then, she went downstairs to start another day of pretend.

That evening, they were to go to a rout at the home of the Dowager Duchess of Ashton. 'It will be tiresome,' Julian said. 'Routs always are.'

'But she has an excellent cook,' Portia said as the got into the carriage. 'And a good cellar. And I like rout cakes.'

'It is hardly a difficult recipe,' Julian grumbled. 'Ask Cook to make you a batch for tea.'

Cassie laughed behind her hand. Then, she asked, 'Why did you accept the invitation?'

'Everyone is going,' Portia said. 'And we want you to be seen at the best places.'

She was tempted to tell them that they could stay home and she would not be bothered. But the carriage was already moving and she had never been to a rout before. When they arrived, it appeared that Portia was right about the number of guests. They were forced to walk the last block to the townhouse, since the driver could not get any closer due to the traffic in the street.

When they reached the door, the footman let them into a foyer that was crowded with people elbow to elbow, chatting amiably and ignoring the press around them. Portia pointed to the left. 'The food is likely to be in that direction. The Duchess is probably to the right.'

Julian, who was tall enough to see over much of the crowd, approached the party as if planning a military campaign. 'Strategically, it would be best to begin at the buffet and let the flow carry us to the Duchess. From there, we can make our farewells and return here. Come, let us get you that rout cake.'

He pushed forward through the throng, and they followed in his wake. Eventually, they reached the food and drink, which they ate while standing, as nearly all the furniture had been removed to make space for more people. Then, they trekked back across the house, stopping occasionally to chat with friends.

Eventually, they arrived in what appeared to be the main receiving room, and the divan at the back where a beautiful woman of uncertain years was holding court over her guests. When she saw Julian, she waved a languid hand, encouraging him to come forward. 'Septon, my dear! And your lovely wife. So good of you to come visit with us.'

Cassie glanced around them to see who she might mean, for there did not seem to be an *us* in residence. Just the Duchess, stretched out on the couch and showing an inappropriate amount of ankle.

'Francesca,' Julian said, bending down to kiss her on both cheeks.

Cassie glanced at Portia whose smile seemed to tighten into something less than genuine, then relax again as her husband stepped away from the Duchess.

Their hostess did not seem to notice, looking past Portia and holding out a hand to Cassie. 'And you must be the lauded Miss Fisk. Come here. Let me see you.'

She stepped forward and curtsied. 'Your Grace.'

'I am soooo sorry,' the Duchess said, shaking her head. 'It must have come as a great shock to you.'

This was baffling. Cassie looked from the Duchess and back to her brother, waiting for an explanation.

Francesca registered her puzzlement and smiled, her eyes glittering. 'You have not heard? Oh, my dear.' Her expression seemed to flicker as if she knew sympathy was called for but could not hide the glee of sharing such a juicy bit of gossip.

'You obviously know something we do not,' Portia said, with exaggerated patience. 'Tell us the news.'

'It is about Mr Andrew Rutland,' she said in a stage whisper that carried halfway across the room. 'His father has gotten wind of his gambling debts and sent him home immediately.' Her eyes grew round. 'Apparently, he owes upward of ten thousand pounds and is dependent on the Earl for his allowance.' She snatched Cassie's hand and patted it vigorously. 'I understand that he was courting you, dear. It is hard, but you have made a narrow escape.'

'Thank you for the information,' Cassie said, drawing her hand back as gently as she could. 'I have indeed avoided catastrophe.'

Then, she looked past them at her next quarry. 'Westbridge! Join us. We are just speaking of Rutland. You have heard, haven't you?'

Cassie turned around to see the Duke approaching. He wore the same guarded smile that Portia did and greeted the Duchess with a shallow bow instead of kisses. 'Francesca.'

'Sebastian,' she said, shifting her leg to reveal a bit more stocking. 'It has been years since you have accepted my invitation.'

'Six,' he replied.

'Have you heard about Rutland?' she said in another loud whisper.

'Indeed,' he replied. 'A very bad business, that.' As Cassie watched, the duke and her brother exchanged glances. Then, they both turned back to the Duchess as if nothing had happened.

But she was focusing her attention on Cassie and Portia. 'It is so good to see the two of them, back together,' she said to Portia. To Cassie, she said, 'They duelled, you know.' She cupped a hand around her mouth, so her whisper would carry. 'Over a woman.'

'Over me, actually,' Portia said with narrowed eyes and a satisfied smile.

Julian took her hand and raised it to his lips. 'To the victor, the spoils.'

'But it was not always thus,' the Duchess said. 'At one time, you were both obsessed with me.' Her grin turned catlike. 'You, particularly, Westbridge.'

His expression changed, turning hard in a way she'd not seen before. 'I am sure Miss Fisk is not interested in tales of your many conquests, Francesca.'

She ignored him and went on. 'It may be hard for you to believe, but Sebastian was the most innocent of boys, back in the day. Still at Oxford, and so studious. He had eyes for nothing but books, back then.'

'That is hardly a surprise,' Cassie said, thinking of the book in his nightstand. 'I understand he still enjoys reading very much.'

Three sets of eyes turned to her, surprised.

Only the Duchess was unmoved and continued with her story. 'I met him on his first trip to London,' she said. 'How old were you then, Sebastian? Twenty?'

'Nineteen,' he snapped. 'My father had just died.'

'As green as fresh-cut grass,' she said, stifling a bored yawn. 'Positively virginal. But that did not last long, did it, darling?'

'But that was quite some time ago,' Portia said, with an equally catlike smile. 'You must have been barely past forty when it happened, Francesca.'

'Thirty-two,' the Duchess replied, her smile disappearing as she looked at Portia.

'I wouldn't know. I was still in the schoolroom at the time,' Portia said, still smiling.

'And on that, I think we'll take our leave,' Julian said, taking his wife by the arm. 'Good evening to you as well, Westbridge.'

'I'll follow you out,' the other man replied, turning to go with them. He walked at their side until they were lost in the crowd, then disappeared.

When he was gone, Julian leaned towards Portia and said, 'You were the one who wanted to come here.'

'Because I do not want it spread around that I am afraid of your old lovers,' she said.

'That was very long ago,' he replied. 'And I thought you enjoyed this party.'

'I said I liked her rout cakes. I did not say I liked her,' Portia replied. Then, she waved her reticule and opened it to show them it contained cake and a folded sheet of paper. 'I have taken several for the ride home and bribed a footman to run to the kitchen and copy out the recipe for me. We do not have to come back next year at all.'

But that meant that Cassie might never hear the end of the story that the Duchess was so eager to tell. They had made their way to the door and Julian had gone to see if he could find their carriage. Cassie used the opportunity to question her sister-in-law.

'The Duchess was very strange,' she began. 'And Westbridge did not seem to like her very much.'

Portia gave her a prim look, and said, 'It is not polite to spread gossip.' Then, she smiled. 'But when it comes to *her*? I am only telling you what everyone knows. And no, Sebastian does not like her very much. She led him a merry chase and he has not forgiven her for it.'

Cassie leaned forward to whisper, 'She said that he was naive when she met him. After all the warnings you have given me about him, I find that hard to believe.'

'We all start life innocent,' Portia reminded her.

'It is not as if he was a rake in the womb. From what I understand, his father died while he was at university, and he came down to London to take up the family seat in Parliament.'

'How sad,' she said.

Portia nodded. 'His mother died when he was born, and he was quite close to his father. The loss hit him hard.'

'And then, he met Francesca?' Cassie said.

'Her husband had died several years before. She was young and beautiful, and paid no mind to the strictures Society placed on her, even before he was gone.'

'How is she still accepted?' Cassie asked, shocked.

'She is not. Not everywhere, at least. But money and a title can smooth over the majority of her sins.'

'And rout cakes?' she said.

'It is a shame that the best cook in London works for such a harpy,' Portia said with a sigh. 'Gentlemen like her better than ladies do. And though her lovers might change from year to year, she is careful to choose men who are assets and not liabilities.'

'And that is why she picked the Duke of Westbridge,' she said, trying not to appear too interested.

'On the contrary, she refused him publicly. He even went so far as to offer marriage. She laughed in his face and told half of London about it.'

Cassie thought of her own public refusal and winced. 'Does he do that often? Offer marriage, I mean.'

'Certainly not. He is a rake not a fool. Making a casual offer to women he wanted to bed would result in a breach of promise lawsuit, and he wants to stay out of the courts.'

'Oh,' Cassie said. She had not considered that.

'But when he met Francesca, he was young and serious and a little full of himself. He offered. And she told him that while another titled husband might be nice, he was too inexperienced to please her.'

'She turned virtue into a vice?' Cassie said shocked.

'And she made sure everyone heard the story,' Portia said. 'Even girls in their first Season were laughing at him.'

Cassie winced. Being new to town, she could still feel the judgement of the people around her and the desire to be accepted. To be loved. 'What did he do?'

'He made himself into the man she wanted. Cold and experienced and old beyond his years. In a single Season, he became one of the most notorious rakes of the *ton*.'

'The next Season?'

'He courted her. She was intrigued, of course. So he led her on, then cast her off, making sure that the jilting was just as public as his had been. From what I understand, it was quite the scandal.'

'It must have been,' Cassie said. It was hard to imagine the Duke as a sweet, young student. But it was much easier to believe he turned bitter in the space of a year. 'And I suppose, once he was done with her, he did not return to his old studiousness?'

'He was sent down from Oxford in what would have been his last year,' she said. 'Public drunkenness, fighting and gambling. Julian has been friends with him since they were in school together and says he can be very clever when he wishes to be. But he is seldom serious, so it is hard to tell.'

'I see,' she said. But before she could press for more information, Julian reappeared to lead them to the carriage.

Chapter Ten

It was just past noon the next day, when Sebastian arrived at White's. After a meal of cold roast beef, cheese and pickle, he settled in the main room and declared it not too early for a brandy. The drink had just arrived, when Julian appeared and took the seat beside him. He signalled the waiter for a glass of his own and said without preamble, 'What did you do to Rutland?'

'Me?' He gave his friend a blank look.

'Do not pretend. You ruined him. How? To what purpose?'

'He ruined himself,' Sebastian said, taking a sip. 'None of the rumours that have been spread about him were lies. And there are juicer stories than a few gambling debts, if you wish to hear them. But they were not necessary to accomplish his removal to the country. Thus, he was spared their revelation.'

'How did you learn of them?'

'Last night at the Ashton rout. Everyone was speaking of it.' He took another sip.

'You would not be caught dead at the Ashton rout without a good reason. You came to spread gossip, not to hear it.'

Sebastian held up his hands in surrender. 'He did not make good on a marker he left at Sally Green's. He is lucky I covered it for him before she sent someone to break his legs. In exchange for the payment, she told me everything there was to hear.'

'Humph.' Julian's drink arrived and he took a long sip. 'That does not answer the why of it.' He gave Sebastian a side-eyed glare. 'What were you doing in the maze at the Montpellier?'

'What does anyone do in the maze at the Montpellier?' he said. The answer was not usually 'spy on others'. But Julian did not need the full truth. He just needed enough to set his mind at rest. 'I heard a lady in distress.'

'Distress?' Julian was frowning, but it was no longer at him.

'Nothing too severe. She said, "No". The man she was with did not respond as he should have. I intervened.'

'Cassandra said nothing of this,' Julian said, his anger turning to worry.

'She was not hurt,' he said hurriedly. 'She was

ashamed, although I told her there was no reason to be. It was not her idea to go into the maze, after all.'

Now it was Julian who was embarrassed, flushing pink as he tried to hide behind his brandy. 'She told me off after you left.'

'Good for her,' Sebastian said, offering a toast to her before drinking again.

'We will have no such trouble with the other man courting her,' Julian said, settling back into his chair.

'Tobias Blake?' Sebastian said, feigning disinterest.

Julian nodded. 'The fellow's reputation is spotless. And it was not my idea that she should entertain his suit.'

'It was her father's,' Sebastian said.

'The Fisks went back to the country after the ball,' Julian said. 'There has been no pressure from them on the matter in some time. And Cassandra still plans to meet with him tomorrow. There will be no funny business because she is taking her maid for a chaperone.'

'It sounds like a delightful outing,' Sebastian said, wrinkling his nose.

'I doubt he will make a proposal at the Royal Menagerie. It is not a particularly romantic place. But then, Blake does not seem to be a particularly romantic individual.'

Although Sebastian had not spoken with Blake, the assessment seemed accurate. Tobias Blake looked dull from a distance, and he did not think a closer inspection would add lustre. Still, there must be some spark in the little clergymen that could be lit. If he wished to kindle it before tomorrow, he had best get about it.

Sebastian checked his watch. 'You must forgive me, Septon. I am late for an appointment.'

'Farewell,' his friend said, and waved him out the door.

It took some time to search out the lodgings of Mr Blake. He was hardly the sort to have a set at The Albany. Nor did he keep rooms in Jermyn Street or St James's. And he had not seen the man at Almack's, so it was unlikely he had connections in Society.

But he had been at the Septon charity ball. Not unusual for a man of the cloth, he supposed. Perhaps he was seeking a job with the school. Or was he a former orphan with a charity education in his past? Either way, Sebastian doubted that the man had any money to speak of.

He could not exactly ask Septon for more information. It was one thing to interfere with a bounder like Rutland. It would not win him points with the

Fisks, Julian or Cassie if he was caught corrupting a clergyman.

But someone had to put a stop to him. Perhaps Cassie's family was not bothered by the thought of such a humble future. But he much preferred thinking of her living in luxury. What was the point of elevating her in Society only to dump her right back into a different vicarage?

It did not matter. He would see to it that it did not happen. What was it Archimedes had said about moving the world with the right lever? There were any number of tools he could use to dislodge Mr Blake from Miss Fisk's side. He had but to find the fellow and pry.

It took some searching through lodging houses and pensions before he discovered Mr Blake in Cheapside, letting a furnished room in a house owned by a widow. When she called her lodger down to the sitting room, he looked to Sebastian as he had at the ball, as if he was in need of a good meal and a good tailor. It would not be hard to find something the little vicar could not resist, for it was clear he had nothing now.

The landlady brought them a tray containing a pot of watery tea and a few slices of thinly buttered bread. Then, she left them alone and closed the door behind her.

Sebastian smiled at the other man, feeling a bit like the devil in *Faust*. He did not exactly want Blake's soul, since he barely had use for his own. He just wanted him to go away. 'Mr Blake,' he said rising and clapping the fellow on the back so forcefully that it knocked his spectacles askew. 'Just the man I was looking for.'

'You were?' Blake straightened his glasses and looked up at him with watery blue eyes. He squinted a bit, confused, and he stepped back to offer a deep and awkward bow. 'I do not believe we have been introduced.' He considered for a moment. 'You are the Duke of Westbridge, are you not?'

'Right in one, Mr Blake,' he said wringing the man's hand. 'I have had the devil of a time finding you. Your lodgings are quite out of the common way.'

'They are?' The man squinted at him again, confused. 'And to what do I owe that honour?'

'I wish,' he said, pausing dramatically, 'to talk to you about your future.'

'My future?'

'Sit down, sit down,' Sebastian said, doing so himself and pouring the tea. 'We have much to discuss.'

'We do?' Blake's expression was utterly guileless and annoyingly devoid of dissipation.

For the moment, at least.

If Sebastian had been a better man, he might feel guilty trying to cheat an innocent. But he was not a better man. There was barely any good in him at all. So he poured a bit of milk into his tea and began to speak.

The next afternoon, Cassie arrived at the Tower of London just at one, excited for the adventure ahead. Paging through the guidebook in her hand, she smiled at Bessie. 'I have always heard of the place but never thought I would be able to visit. When I was a girl in the country, I would read myself to sleep on the descriptions of the animals.'

'I have been many a time,' the maid said, smiling. 'It is quite grand. Even better when you can see it with a beau.'

'Well, yes. I suppose.' Would it be wrong to admit that she was much more excited to see a live tiger than she was to see Tobias Blake? There was nothing really wrong with him. But neither was there anything very right.

That was being unfair. He had many good qualities. He was honourable. Unlike Mr Rutland he was never going to be the topic of conversation at a party. No one would talk about him at all. Ever. Even she was struggling to find something to say.

Unless it was to announce that he wasn't punctual. He had said he would meet her at one, but there was no sign of him outside. In case he was waiting inside, they walked through the courtyard and up the stairs towards the place where the animals were kept.

But when she reached the arch painted with a lion, a man's hand reached past her and rang the bell to summon the keeper.

She turned with a smile, expecting Mr Blake. She was surprised to see the Duke of Westbridge smiling back at her. 'Miss Fisk,' he said, offering a bow. 'How delightful to see you again.'

'What are you doing here?' she said trying not to gasp. 'How did you find me?'

'Your little friend the cleric mentioned that he would be meeting you today,' he said. 'I thought I might join you.'

'You spoke to him?' she said, her eyes narrowing.

'Just yesterday. We had a lovely conversation. Most informative.'

'What about?' she said, with a sinking feeling in the pit of her stomach.

'His plans for the future,' he said, looking up towards the ceiling as if he could see heaven and all its angels were dancing on the roof.

'What did you do to him?' she said, hands on hips and stepping forward to block his way. It was quite all right that he'd found a way to get rid of Andrew Rutland. But Mr Blake had done nothing wrong.

Not yet, at least.

'Do? To him?' He pointed to himself and looked around. 'You think I would interfere with the man's goals?'

'If it suited you? Or if he'd crossed you in some way?' Which he certainly would have, if Sebastian was intent on courting her. 'In fact,' she said with a look of even deeper suspicion, 'I think you would torture the poor man, just because it amused you to do so.'

His eyes widened, and he laid a hand on his heart as if ready to swear. 'You seriously think so little of me?'

'In a word? Yes. Now, where is he?'

He checked his watch. 'Several miles out to sea by now, I should think. The ship left at nine this morning.'

She stared at him in horror. 'Get him back. Return him here, immediately, or I shall…' What should she do? She had no idea. A thought occurred to her. 'I shall talk to someone in the navy and tell them they have press-ganged an innocent citizen.'

He laughed long and hard, reaching into his pocket for a handkerchief to wipe his streaming eyes. 'You think I have waylaid him? Sent him to the Americas, perhaps? Oh, my dear, you have a lurid imagination. Mr Blake is in the finest cabin available and on his way to the Holy Lands on a pilgrimage of faith.'

'He is what?'

'He expressed a desire to see Jerusalem before he died. I told him that life was short and there was no time like the present. Then I supplied him with the necessary funds and put him on a boat and with a promise of a living on my lands upon his return.'

'On your lands?'

'The church in the village has been unoccupied for some time.' He blinked innocently. 'I admit that I have been somewhat remiss in seeing to that.'

'Because you are a blackguard and a villain,' she said, glaring at him.

'What have I done to you that would give you such an opinion of me?' he said, smiling expectantly.

He'd plied her with pornography, then pulled her into his bed and kissed her. Not that she wanted to admit the fact with Bessie standing right there. Or at all. Owning their shared past was one step closer to admitting that she could not forget how pleasant it had been to be held in his arms.

And since meeting him again?

He had rescued her from Rutland, proposed marriage, given her flowers and a pin… And tricked her into waltzing. His recent behaviour was hardly the work of a scoundrel.

But he was still staring at her, waiting for an answer.

'Everyone knows you for what you are,' she sputtered. 'And Julian says you are not to be trusted.'

'His assessment of my character is accurate,' he said, after a moment's reflection. 'I have much to repent for. But not this.' He reached into his pocket and withdrew a letter. 'I told Blake I would deliver his apologies. Time was short. And since I meant to see you anyway I had him write you a note.'

She snatched the paper from his hand, tore the seal and read.

It was just as he said, a brief note to tell her he was sorry that he could not meet with her because of a marvellous and unexpected opportunity. It went on for several lines, extolling the generosity and kindness of the Duke, before closing with a wish for her continued good health and good fortune in her search for a husband.

She stared at the paper, pretending to read it again while she searched for a response more appropriate than her true feelings. Tobias Blake was a good man. A decent man. If he had not been waylaid by Westbridge, he might have offered for her this very afternoon and ended her husband hunting.

But, when presented by what should have been a crushing disappointment, all she could think was, *Thank God, he is gone.*

Was there something wrong with her, that she did not want to marry? Or was there something wrong with the men who were interested in her?

Andrew would not have suited. She did not want to wed a gambler. But she had been preparing to reject him well before that scandal had broken.

And there was nothing wrong with Tobias. He was stable, trustworthy and hardworking. Her whole family would have been overjoyed if she'd have accepted his offer. As a husband, he would have been perfectly…

Adequate.

Boring.

I am a horrible person.

'You are a horrible person,' she blurted, staring at the Duke as she folded up the paper and stuffed it in her reticule. If it were not for Westgate and his waltzing and flirting and bogus offers of marriage, she would not be having these terrible thoughts.

'Horrible,' he said, considering. 'I fail to see why you would think so in this case. I gave the man the thing he wanted most in the world. Do you not find that generous of me?'

'Why did you do it?' she demanded.

'Altruism?' He continued to smile, offering an open-handed gesture to show he had nothing to hide.

'You did him a favour. But it was not out of the goodness of your heart,' she said. 'You are the first to admit that you have no goodness there. Do not spoil what must be a rare, charitable act by lying about it.' She folded her arms and waited.

He dropped his hands, then folded them behind his back. 'A tour such as he wishes will take three weeks at least, with additional time for travel, prayer and the purchase of souvenirs. It will be more than a month before we see him again.'

'We?' she said.

'You,' he admitted.

She fought back the feelings of relief, and waited for him to continue.

'He is interested in you,' he said. 'Or, rather, he is interested in a position with your brother's school, or a living on his property.'

'There is nothing wrong with that,' she said, trying not to be hurt by the blunt assessment. 'He is to be admired for his ambition, and his beneficent nature.'

'But it is not very flattering, is it? Wouldn't you prefer to marry a man who was interested in you?'

'We were not discussing marriage.' They hadn't needed to. It was assumed. Inevitable. Inescapable.

'I have only known him for a week,' she said, frightened by how quickly things were moving.

'And now, you will know him for over a month before a decision is made in his favour,' he said with a superior nod. 'Perhaps he will write to you while he is gone to tell you of his travels. Or perhaps not.'

'And what am I to do in the meantime?' she said, wondering if he was going to propose again. Right now, she did not want to marry anyone.

'Anything you like,' he said. 'You could visit the menagerie with me, if you wanted to. If your interest in nature extends to the larger animals, you must be looking forward to it. We are here already, and it is a shame to waste the opportunity.'

'Even though you put a stranger on a boat to Jerusalem so that you could stalk me without interference?'

'Jaffa,' he corrected her. 'Jerusalem has no port.'

She doubted he'd learned that fact while studying the Bible. It was just one small detail in some greater plan that seemed to involve her. 'I am not going to swoon into your arms just because there is no other man present,' she said, trying to read his response.

'Neither will you rush to a decision in Blake's favour, simply because he showed the minimum attention to you,' he responded. 'Your father would likely approve of such a match, as would your brother. Mr

Blake is utterly toothless and no threat to you in any way.' He looked at her again as if considering.

'Because he is a good man.'

'I never said he wasn't. I'd rather thought that, when tempted he would choose something a little less pious. Filthy lucre perhaps. But he proved virtuous, right to the bone.'

'And you mock him because of it,' she said, annoyed.

'Not at all. He wants to serve the Lord and help his people. I have no problem with that. It should be encouraged in others, so the rest of us don't have to be bothered with it.'

'You have no interest in performing good works?'

'That is not precisely true either,' he said, considering for a minute. 'I contribute to the care of widows and orphans and have my favourite charities, as every man of means should. But I see no need to make a show of it. The Lord knows my character even better than the *ton* does. If I have not done enough with my life, He will tell me when I pass.' Then, he smiled, supremely confident in his answer, as he seemed to be in all things.

This was a surprise. She had thought him selfish and superficial. But there seemed to be depths to him that he refused to show to others. But that did not justify his being here. He wanted something from her. He simply hadn't asked for it, yet.

'I suppose now you will tell me that you are just as good a man as Mr Blake.'

'Not a better man,' he said. 'Merely a different one.'

'And with a sudden desire to see the animals in the menagerie?' she said.

'Not particularly. I have seen them before,' he said.

'Then, this will be quite dull for you.'

'I have never seen you, seeing them,' he said. 'That will make the experience a novelty for me.'

She had no idea how to respond to this. With all the women he had known, she suspected she was the least novel of the bunch.

But he took her silence as acceptance and paid the shillings necessary for admittance. Then, the keeper led the three of them past the many cages, telling them of the origins of the animals and their feeding and care.

At first, it was a relief to think of something other than her own future. There were a great many lions, chewing on bones and staring listlessly back at her from behind the bars. The leopard was pacing nervously from one side of her cage to the other and seemed bothered by the screams of the eagle, that flapped its wings frantically but did not have the space to fly.

The keeper was particularly proud of a black leopardess named Miss Nancy, pointing out the spots still visible in her black-on-black velvety fur. As they stood watching her, she came to the bars and stared back at Cassie, slowly blinking her golden eyes which were filled with a deep sadness.

Probably because Miss Nancy did not want to end her life in a cage. At some point in the past, she'd been roaming free in the jungle where the air and the food were fresh, and every day was new and different. Her keeper might dote on her and extoll her virtues to each person that passed the cage which held her. But he was a jailer, nothing more than that.

Cassie felt a sudden rush of melancholy and a tightness in her chest, as if her ribs were the bars of a cage and her heart was pounding to get out. The tears blurred her vision until all she could see was the glow of those sad, gold eyes staring into hers as if begging for rescue.

Finally, she could stand no more and turned away.

The Duke noticed immediately and touched her arm, concerned.

She shook her head and whispered, 'It is so sad.'

'How so?' he asked staring down at her.

'That such a majestic creature will never know

freedom. She and her friends were designed by the Lord to run wild in the jungle. To hunt and play…'

'And mate,' he suggested, which shouldn't have surprised her.

But he was right. 'To have more of their kind. To live and die under the open sky. But instead, the poor things are trapped here so that we can gape at them. Fed on dead meat. Even the kitchen cat has more freedom.' She reached for the handkerchief in her reticule and wiped her eyes.

The Duke was faster, offering her his. 'You have a tender heart,' he said.

She glanced around her at Bessie and the other visitors, who seemed to be enjoying the show, and muttered, 'You must think me quite provincial.'

'Not at all,' he replied. 'To care so deeply about helpless animals is an admirable quality.' Then, he smiled. 'I knew a girl very like you once, willing to walk into the den of a miserable beast and ease his suffering.'

'I am not that brave,' she said, glancing back at the leopardess. 'I do not think I can bear this a moment longer.'

'Let me take you out of here,' he said, and turned to Bessie. 'There is no reason you cannot stay and enjoy the sights. I will not take your mistress any farther than the courtyard.'

The girl gave him a doubtful look, which lessened when he produced a gold coin from his pocket. 'I mean no harm. I simply do not wish her to be unhappy.'

She hesitated a moment longer, then took the coin and turned her back on them.

Cassie looked helplessly at her, knowing that she should refuse. But at the moment, she was tired of London and all the foolishness connected to it. She needed air as much as these cats did.

For all she knew, the Duke was no more interested in her future happiness than the rest of the men she'd met. But he was at least willing to help her right now. So she took his arm and let him lead her down the stairs and out into the open air outside the tower.

Once there, he led her along one of the walls to a bench, sitting down beside her as she turned her face up to catch the sun so her tears would dry. It was better here, but not as nice as her little house in St John's Wood. And definitely not the same as the country had been. 'The air is not so fresh as it is at home,' she said with a sigh.

'The misfortunes of living in a city,' he agreed. 'I do not often go home to my estate. But I must admit, it is very peaceful there. Very clean.'

She glanced over at him. 'Why do you not spend more time there?'

'It is lonely as well,' he admitted. 'My grandmother died over a year ago and I have no family left. I do not feel it so much when I am in town. But when I go back to the manor? I am alone with my memories and conscious of the loss.' His smile had disappeared and he stared down at his feet, scuffing at the dirt with the toe of his boot as if trying to erase the past.

He was so rarely serious that the change surprised her. But the way he looked now felt raw and real. He was in pain, just as he'd been when she'd nursed him and did not have the strength to conceal his intentions with a wink and a grin.

He looked to her again, and his smile returned, though it was sadder than before. 'Now you are looking at me as you did those cats. I am not as hopeless as that.' Then he added, 'At least, not anymore.'

Which meant he had been hopeless once. Or perhaps more than once. She thought of what Portia had told her after the rout. 'May I ask you a question?' she said, trying to catch his eye.

He looked up, puzzled, then said, 'Whatever you wish.'

'When you were at Oxford, what was your favourite subject?'

The question seemed to surprise him. Then, he looked down again as if embarrassed. 'I did not actually complete my course of studies.'

'So I have been told,' she said, dipping her head, as well.

When he looked up, his usual sardonic smile had returned. 'It was decided that, if I meant to study barmaids and dice and general drunkenness, I would be better off doing graduate studies in London.'

'An interesting way to describe expulsion,' she said, and waited for a better answer.

'I had left the university in spirit long before I was asked to physically depart. It hardly seems fair to blame the dean for coming late to a conclusion that I had already arrived at.' He gave a small nod as if hoping that it would put an end to the questions about the past.

'But I am interested in the time before you left. Before the barmaids and the dice and the drinking. I assume there was a time when you took your studies seriously.'

'Why would you think such a thing?' he asked, giving her an intense look meant to make her squirm just as her questions seemed to affect him.

She stared back at him, struggling to hide her discomfort. 'Why would I not? I have heard that it was not until your final year that you were sent down.

It stands to reason that you did something with the years before.'

'You have heard?' he said, raising an eyebrow. 'Why, Miss Fisk, have you been asking after me?'

'Perhaps,' she admitted. 'But now, I am asking you directly. What was your course of study?'

He seemed to try and reject various responses in his head before speaking, as if seeking something that was more clever than the truth. Then, he surrendered and said, 'Moral philosophy and ethics.' Then, he gave her a worried look, as he waited for her response.

He was probably afraid she would laugh. Instead, she smiled and nodded.

'You are not surprised?' he said.

'Cynics are nothing more than optimists who have known too much disappointment,' she replied. 'It makes perfect sense to me that a rake might be made from a disenchanted ethicist.'

'That is probably true,' he said, as if he had never considered it. 'It did seem, at the time, that high standards and upright behaviour gained me very little.'

'Probably because you were seeking the wrong things,' she said, thinking of the Duchess of Ashton.

'Now you sound like a vicar's daughter,' he replied.

'Because that is what I am,' she said with a wave of her hand. 'Tell me, did a change in character achieve your goals?'

He hesitated again, then admitted, 'The woman I sought to impress no longer interested me. Why have one woman when I could have a dozen, each prettier than the last?'

'Your heart was not engaged,' she said.

'It does not do to think with one's heart, when one lives the way I do. The less one feels, the better.'

'I see.' But really, she did not. The statement did not tell her what, if anything, he felt for her.

'That is not to say I am incapable of feeling,' he said quickly, as if sensing her confusion. 'It is just that I have lost too many people not to be cautious. I never knew my mother. She died when I was born. My father was gone before I came of age. And my grandmother…'

He paused and swallowed before continuing. 'The poor woman had great hopes for me. She died disappointed.' He was staring at his feet again, his expression bleak.

'I recall seeing the notice of her death in the newspaper,' she said gently.

He did not look up. 'It was shortly before the duel. I was still in a funk about it when I quarrelled with Septon.'

'You must have been very fond of her,' she said.

'She was fond of me, more like,' he said with a short laugh. 'When my father did not remarry, she took it upon herself to help with the raising of me until I went off to school. She loved me, even as I dragged the family name through the dirt. I did not deserve her affection. I lied to her nearly every time I saw her. Told her the gossip she'd heard about me was nothing more than exaggeration.'

'And was it?'

'No. No, it wasn't. But in our visits, we both preferred to maintain the fantasy.' He looked up, his brow furrowed. 'She was lying, as well. Pretending to believe me. She told me so, near the end. She said it was about time that I grew into my rank and stopped being such an ass.'

'Perhaps she was right,' Cassie said.

'I agreed at the time,' he said. 'I promised that when next she saw me, I would be a changed man.'

'I am sure the promise made her very happy,' she said.

'And I am equally sure she saw it for the lie it turned out to be,' he said with a bitter smile. 'She summoned me on the night she died. She sent a messenger with a letter asking me to come to dinner. He was to wait for my response. I was planning to go gaming with Septon and end the night with my mistress. So, I fobbed the old lady off with some excuse about a late session of Parliament.' His voice gave a surprising crack and he took a moment to steady himself before speaking again. 'I knew she followed the news closely. She was well aware that no such thing was happening. It was her last night, and I would not even take the time to lie properly, much less keep my promise or accept her invitation.' He fell silent, lost in the past.

She could not think of a response, either. Her father would know what to do in a case like this. He always seemed to have the right words when people were hurting, as Sebastian clearly was. She reached out a hand and took his. 'I think you underestimate her. She loved you. And falling out of love with you is harder than you may think.' Then, she touched his chin and turned his face to her for a kiss.

It was nothing, really. Just a touch of their lips. Over before it had begun and with none of the passion that they'd shared a year ago. But it was a kiss, all the same. And she had been the one to give it.

She looked around her, sure she must be blushing furiously for her skin felt hot and prickly as if she'd sat for hours in the sun. There were few people about and none that she knew. With luck, none of them recognized her, either. She turned back to the Duke who was pink, as well. 'Why, Miss Fisk,' he said, with wide eyes and a slowly dawning smile.

'I should not have done that,' she said, placing her fingertips on her lips.

'Too late for regrets,' he said, staring at her mouth. 'And you must call me Sebastian, when we speak of this again.'

'We will not,' she said. 'Speak of it, that is.'

'Shall I tell your brother that you are toying with my affections?' he said, fanning himself with his hand.

'Don't you dare,' she whispered, turning to look straight ahead as if she could pretend he did not exist.

'Oh, ho, ho,' he said, slapping his knees in delight. 'If I were you, I would not take that tone, Cassandra Fisk. You must be much nicer to me if you wish me to keep quiet.'

'You are horrible,' she said, scowling. Why had she forgotten the fact? Bessie was just coming out of the doorway that led to the menagerie and would be with them in moments, and she didn't want the Duke talking casually of blackmail in front of her maid.

'Call me Sebastian,' he coaxed. 'Say, "You are horrible Sebastian".'

'You are,' she whispered. 'Horrible. Sebastian.'

'But I will meet you, tomorrow in Hyde Park at two in the afternoon,' he added, with a placid smile.

She let out a moan of frustration.

'I would hurry,' he said softly. 'Your maid is almost here, and it will take a promise to seal my lips.'

'Tomorrow,' she said. 'Hyde Park. But I am not coming alone.'

'Bring Bessie,' he said, waving to the maid. As she arrived at their side, he stood and took her by the hands, swinging her around until she laughed and pushing her down onto the bench beside her mistress. 'I am sure she will welcome the exercise. But for now?' He pulled off his hat and swept it before him in a theatrical bow. 'Fare thee well, ladies. Until tomorrow.' Then, he strolled off down the path, whistling.

Chapter Eleven

'Still not right. Something simple, perhaps.'

Sebastian ripped the complicated cravat from around his throat and tossed it on the floor.

His valet, Jenks, sighed and pulled a third linen from the wardrobe then turned back to his master. 'Perhaps I might suggest something, Your Grace.' By the look in his eyes, what he wanted to suggest was a length of plain hemp and a short drop. Jenks was a patient man, but he had his limits.

'She kissed me,' Sebastian said, giving the servant a desperate look.

This was met with a blank stare, as if to remind him that he'd kissed half the women in London, and it did not normally result in so much wasted linen.

'You don't understand,' he said. '*She* kissed *me*.'

Jenks blinked once, shocked. Then, he turned back to the bureau. 'I suggest black silk.'

'For evening?' Sebastian said, equally surprised.

'Very Byronic. But tied in a *sentimentale* to give it a touch of youthful whimsy.'

'Interesting,' Sebastian said, almost nodding in approval until a cautioning grunt from Jenks reminded him that movement now would spoil the knot. Once this was properly done and he had been helped into his evening coat, he had to admit that the valet was right. He looked elegant, but distinctive.

It was exactly what he wanted if he was to stand out from the crowd at the Theatre Royal, tonight. When he'd seen the playbill, he had not needed to bribe a Septon maid to know where the family would be tonight. The entr'acte soprano was a favourite of both Portia and Julian's and he doubted they would leave Cassie behind.

Since their box was directly across from his, he could have a delightful evening of gazing at her and, with luck, a chance meeting in the saloon leading to their seats.

He sighed and smiled. He had been smitten before. But after this afternoon, he was quite lost to her. The first thing he'd seen upon arriving at the menagerie was the pin he'd given her, tucked into the flowers on her bonnet as if it had crawled there itself. She was wearing the thing as if it had greater meaning to her than some random trinket. It gave him hope.

And what had she said before the kiss? That it was hard to fall out of love with him? The implications of that were almost too wonderful to believe. Though she was resisting the truth, her feelings had not changed. She was still his, just as he was hers. It was only loyalty to her brother that was keeping her from surrender.

She was weakening, he was sure. She had come close to admitting her feelings today. If he could get her away from her keepers, somewhere they might be truly alone, the last barriers between them would fall. He patted the breast pocket of his coat where he kept his mother's wedding ring, a beaded gold band edged in repoussé leaves.

Which would be better, he wondered, to seduce her at the first sign of acceptance, or to wait the excruciating days or weeks until the knot was tied? Or should he let her choose, torturing him as she saw fit until he had expiated every past sin and proved himself worthy?

The thought of their future left him giddy and he gave Jenks a daffy smile and a wave of farewell before setting out for the theatre.

By the time he had settled in his box, the performance had already begun. A Shakespeare comedy, which was a relief. He was in the mood to see lovers united and happy, not a stage strewn with bodies.

But more than anything, he was interested in the box across the circle from him, which was still empty.

It was several more minutes before Septon and his party arrived, filed into the box and took their seats. Cassie was there, of course, wearing an evening gown of silver net that he had not seen before. The colour would suit her grey eyes, he was sure. He could imagine them sparkling as she laughed at something happening on the stage.

Then, the door to the box opened again and another man entered, taking the seat beside her.

Gerald Balard.

Sebastian leaned back in his seat, wishing he could shrink back into the shadows and out of notice. He had seen Balard dancing with her at Almack's and thought nothing of it. She'd danced with dozens of men this Season and had said nothing about this one. Nor had Julian mentioned him as a possible husband.

There had been only two suitors and he'd gotten rid of both of them. The way had been clear for him. Until tonight, and the sudden appearance of this interloper.

Of all the men in London, why did it have to be this one? Balard had the build and good looks of Rutland, with broad shoulders and an excess of wavy brown hair, but none of that man's vices. He was not quite as pure-hearted as Blake. But he did not gamble or drink to excess. And he was wealthier than those two men combined. Distantly related to both an earl and a marquis but able to support himself with his own investments.

If he was here tonight, it had nothing to do with seeking favours from the Duke of Septon. He wanted nothing from Julian, but his sister.

As he watched, Balard leaned towards Cassie, murmuring something into her ear and pointing towards the stage. She smiled and nodded, consulting her programme, and making some comment in return.

They made a lovely couple. If she had been his sister, he'd have been over the moon at the prospect of such a match. She would be guaranteed a future that was comfortable, safe and scandal free.

He should go. She had not noticed him, yet. He could slink away without being seen and meet her tomorrow, as planned. Then he could ask her about her evening. Or, better yet, he could say nothing at all and focus on the events of the afternoon. It was one thing to spy on her and another to get caught doing so in such an obvious way for the hours it would take for this performance to end.

Then, the door to his box opened and a woman slipped in to take the seat beside him.

He turned to see Harriette Wilson smiling and fluttering her fan. 'Westbridge,' she said, her voice a seductive purr. 'I could not bear to see you looking so lonely. I had to come and rescue you.'

'Harriette,' he said. And then, his voice failed him. Harriette Wilson was the most notorious courtesan in London and had her own reserved box, just down the circle from him. It would not be the first time they had enjoyed a performance together.

And after, they had enjoyed far more than that. She was infamous and deserved every bit of her reputation. Someday, he might wish to reminisce about that time.

Just, not now.

'Harriette,' he said, plastering a smile on his face. 'I was not expecting company.'

She gave him a dubious look and draped an arm along the back of his chair, leaning closer. 'Then this is your lucky night,' she said, letting out a puff of breath that ruffled his hair.

'I wouldn't want to interfere with your plans,' he said, leaning away.

'I have nothing tonight,' she said, inching closer until she had almost pushed him off his chair.

'Or offend your protector,' he added, leaning back over the arm of his chair.

'I have no one at the moment,' she said, walking her fingers up the buttons of his vest.

He snatched her hand away, holding it for a moment. 'Flattering though your offer is, I cannot accept.' He sat up straight again, even though it brought him closer to her. Then, he whispered, 'There is a lady I do not wish to disappoint.'

'How interesting,' she said, refusing to move. 'Tell me more.'

'There is not much to tell,' he admitted. 'I have made no offer as yet. But I have no room in my heart for another.'

'True love,' she said with a mischievous smile. 'How delightful. And how rare.' She slid back to her own chair, clasping their joined hands with her free one. 'I will accept your refusal. Tonight, at least. And give you my best wishes.' Then, she leaned forward again and kissed him on the cheek.

He smiled, relieved. Then, he glanced across the theatre and saw the shocked face of Cassie Fisk staring back at him.

Balard was still at her side, leaning close, whispering and pointing at Harriette. Julian and Portia were looking at him as well, their expressions grim and disapproving. If Cassie was not already learning the identity of Sebastian's friend, she would hear of it on the way home.

But it appeared it was already too late for him. She gave him a final frown, then turned deliberately towards the stage, watching the comedy in stony silence.

The play seemed to go on for ages.

There were singers and musicians between the acts, and the farce that followed the main performance. And through it all, Gerald was yammering in her ear about everyone around them, as if they had come to watch the audience, and not the actors. Why was he bothering? She saw these same people at every ball and dinner. Was it really worthy of comment if they wore the same clothing twice in a week?

She had not wanted to bring an escort to the theatre. This evening was supposed to be just the three of them, enjoying Shakespeare and a soprano that Portia assured her was particularly good. But at the last minute, they'd met Mr Balard in the grand saloon, and he'd invited himself to join their party.

And now, she was trapped, smiling politely and being forced to attend to the needs of a gentleman when she only wanted to relax and think about her day

Her hand stole to the amber pin, hidden amongst the silk roses clustered at the top of her bodice. It was a single spot of gold on the silver gown, only noticeable if one took the time to look for it.

Gerald had spotted it, of course. She suspected he was more interested in the breasts concealed beneath it. Or perhaps he was really that interested in women's fashion. He had leaned a little too close and announced she had 'a canker in the fragrant rose'.

When she had not responded, he'd added. 'That is Shakespeare.'

'A sonnet,' she'd agreed. 'Ninety-five, I believe.'

'And it is not really a canker. It is a bug,' he'd added, still staring at her bosom.

'An ant,' she'd clarified.

'It is a curious bit of glitter for such a lovely girl,' he'd said, remembering a moment too late that he should be looking into her eyes.

'It was a gift,' she'd said.

'You wear it out of charity for the giver?' His smile had turned patronizing.

'I wear it because I like it,' she'd said, then she'd stared expectantly at him until he'd given up and turned his attention back to critiquing the crowd.

She'd allowed herself to do so, as well. It had taken only a moment to spot Westbridge in a box across the way. She'd had to struggle to stay focused on the performance and allowed herself only an occasional hungry glance in his direction as she scanned the rest of the people and feigned interest in Mr Balard's never-ending commentary.

'Now, that is interesting,' he'd said, with a disapproving huff.

She'd spared him a polite glance to show that she cared.

He'd pointed, which was exceptionally rude. 'Westbridge has a new light o' love.'

Her head had snapped back to stare at the woman in his box.

'Harriette Wilson,' he'd said smugly. 'I can't fault his taste. She is expensive enough. But she has lain with half the peerage already.'

Cassie stared at the woman, who had all but draped herself over the Duke and was whispering into his ear. 'She is attractive, I suppose. But her nose is a trifle too long.'

Portia had looked at her with narrowed eyes, then raised the little spyglass she carried for a better look.

'It is not her nose that men are interested in,' Julian said, and his wife struck him in the arm with the spyglass before turning to look at the stage again.

Cassie had as well, though she had not heard a word of the play for the rest of the night.

Now they were in the carriage, on the way home again, and she fiddled with the pin on her bodice and stared out the window at the dimly lit streets.

'Mr Balard seemed very nice,' Portia said with a rising inflection as if daring Cassie to comment.

When she did not, Julian said, 'His pedigree is excellent.' Then, he waited with the same thinly veiled interest as Portia did.

She turned and looked from one expectant face to another. 'Next, I suppose you will tell me he has good wind and sound legs.'

'Well,' Portia began cautiously, 'His legs are rather fine.'

Julian gave her a sharp look.

'Some men pad them,' she said with a smile and a shrug. 'He does not.' Then, she looked back to Cassie. 'But beauty is a fleeting virtue. It is more important that he be of good character.'

'And he is that,' her brother assured her. 'There is no scandal attached to his name or his family. He is loosely connected to two titles, though unlikely to inherit them. Wealthy, as well. He just purchased some fine horses at Tattersalls, and a new carriage.'

'He has informed me,' Cassie said, gazing out the window again.

'I am only telling you so that you know I approve,' Julian said, a little more gently.

'And I am telling you that his favourite topics of conversation are other people and himself,' she said. 'The horses were a close third.' Then, because she could not help herself, she added, 'And who is Harriette Wilson?'

There was an awkward pause as Julian and Portia exchanged glances. Then, Julian said, 'As you said just now, it is rude to speak of other people. Especially women like her.'

'Wellington's mistress,' Portia said, then looked at Julian and shrugged. 'And your brother is right. We shouldn't speak of her. Ladies aren't supposed to know such things.'

'And yet, it is clear that they all do,' Cassie said, disgusted. 'I don't know what I dislike more about the people of London, their despicable behaviour, or the lies they tell to hide it.'

Or the way they could seem like the sweetest most misunderstood man on Earth, and then, just a few hours later, act exactly the way everyone assured one that they would. She would meet him tomorrow for the last time and tell him what she thought of him. Then, she would return his stick pin and take the next mail coach back to the Cotswolds.

Chapter Twelve

At five past two the next day, Sebastian was waiting at Hyde Park corner, trying and failing to hide his nervousness. With each minute that passed he grew more sure that Cassie was not coming. Or worse yet, that she would arrive on Balard's arm and offer nothing more than a chilly smile as she passed him.

He had hoped to speak with her after the play, to explain that the brief visit from Harriette had meant nothing. She was an old friend, albeit a very close old friend. Too close, perhaps. Judging by the look she had given him, Balard had told her far too much already.

It was another five minutes before Cassie arrived, alone except for her maid.

'Miss Fisk,' he said with a formal bow. 'How delightful to see you. It is a delightful day as well, is it not?'

'Indeed, Your Grace,' she replied, looking past him into the park.

He stepped into her line of sight so she could not ignore him. 'May I escort you along the Serpentine?'

'That would be most kind of you, Your Grace,' she said, without smiling.

They walked in silence until they reached the keeper's lodge, where he bought a bag of corn for Bessie and sent her off to feed the swans in the water. Then he found a bench for the two of them and invited Cassie to sit.

She did so and fumbled in her reticule for a moment before withdrawing her clenched hand and holding it out to him.

He placed his open hand beneath it, puzzled.

'I have come to return this,' she said, dropping the amber stick pin into his palm.

'No,' he said, automatically.

She looked at him with a raised eyebrow, as if challenging him to disagree.

He took her hand and pressed the pin back into it. 'I will not accept it. You are not even sure where it came from, are you?'

'I think we both know perfectly well,' she said.

'There was no signature on the note. Nothing that anyone can reproach you with. And the pin is a simple thing. There is no obligation attached to it.

It was meant as a token of friendship and you can keep it as such. If your heart is pledged to another, tuck it away in your jewel case and take it out on days when you are feeling sentimental and want to remember the past.'

She was silent, giving him ample time to regret his words. What sort of a fool was he to let her go like this, without a struggle? He should be apologizing, even though he'd done nothing.

Not recently, at least.

And he could not exactly say he was sorry for the things he'd done before he met her. It was far too late to take them back.

Slowly, she closed her hand around the pin and put it back in her purse. Then, she said, 'My heart is not pledged to anyone.'

He let out a sigh of relief.

'Not yet, at least.'

He clutched his heart and pantomimed a mortal wound. 'You took pleasure in that.' Then he held out a hand to her and shook his head. 'I suppose I deserve it. I tortured you, when we first met. Remember the book in my night table?'

'I…' She stopped before she could say more. But she remembered. He knew she did. The same blush stained her cheek now as it did the day he'd tricked her into reading from *Fanny Hill*.

He leaned forward, ready for her next words.

'I have no idea what you are talking about,' she said, thoughts gathered and defenses raised again.

'Of course not,' he said, his smile turning smug. 'I forgot that we have never met until just last week. You could not possibly be the woman whose lips were so sweet I have not stopped thinking about them for over a year.'

'If…this woman was so special to you,' she said cautiously, 'you were not thinking of her last night at the theatre.'

'You are speaking of Harriette Wilson,' he said. 'I have not visited with her or any other woman since before the duel.'

'It did not look that way,' she said glaring at him.

'I cannot help the way it looked,' he said. 'I can only give you my word as a gentleman that what I said is true.'

She snorted.

It hurt. But he should not have been surprised. No one else in London had believed his change in character, either.

'The woman I knew a year ago would have believed in me,' he said softly. 'She saw things in me that I could no longer see in myself.'

She met his gaze, now, her familiar grey eyes staring into his as they had done when he'd first kissed her. The woman who had loved him back to life was still there, hiding inside the cynical beauty. He had to find a way to reach her.

'I would give anything to get her back,' he said. 'Even if just for an hour. She departed so suddenly I did not get her direction. And she left something that I am sure was quite precious to her.'

'Her innocence?' Cassie replied. But there was a breathless quality behind the sharp words as if she wanted to be that woman, as well.

'No,' he said, rummaging in the pocket of his coattail. 'Her Bible.'

Before she could stop it, her hand was rising to take it from him. Then, she jerked it back down, clasping both hands in her lap, lacing the fingers tightly to stifle the urge.

'I am sure it has great sentimental value to her, whoever she was. It is inscribed inside the cover.' He opened it and held it out so she could see as he read. 'To our loving daughter, with all prayers and blessings. Father and Mother.' He glanced over at her, waiting.

She bit her lip.

'I am sure she is missing it. I would most like to return it.'

'Before it catches flames in your hands, you devil.'

He smiled, for there was a time when he'd have

accepted such an insult as a badge of honour. 'It is rather a surprise that both it and I are unscathed.' He closed the cover again and watched as she stared at it, wavering between the truth and the lie she wanted to maintain.

Was she still so afraid that her brother would learn what she had done? Or was she terrified of admitting that she might feel something for him?

Either way, it was cruel to torture her. He did not have the heart to do so any longer. He held the book out to her. 'I suggest you hold it.' When she didn't take it, he urged it on her, pressing it between her clasped hands. 'Please, for the safety of all concerned. Such a valuable item is better in the hands of a vicar's daughter.'

Then, he could not resist a final jab. 'You are pure of spirit and would never lie. Take it and tell me it does not belong with you.'

She glared at him, still silent. She stared down at the book and the frown faded into something sweet and sad. 'If you insist, I will keep it for you.' Then, she seemed to rally, her smile returning. 'If you should need it back, for any reason, to improve your character perhaps…'

He laughed again. 'I will know where to find it.'

'Thank you.' It was not exactly the admission he'd hoped for. But there was nothing mocking in the words. Her hand rested on the spine of the Bible like a caress.

He stared at it for a moment, remembering her, in his room, holding the book just as she was now. She could not hide the woman she was, gentle, caring, and so very different from the women he was used to in London.

He looked away. 'It is nothing.' He slapped his knees and rose, turning back to her and making a deep bow. 'And now, dear lady, your maid has used up her bird feed and is coming back to protect you. I have taken enough of your time. I will see you again soon.'

'I am afraid you will,' she agreed.

He could feel her watching as he walked away.

Once he was out of sight, Cassie set the Bible aside and reached into her reticule to get the pin, fixing it back on her spencer. Last night, she'd been sure that she never wanted to see the Duke of Westbridge again. But today, he had been so kind that she could not imagine a life without him.

She greeted Bessie with a moan of frustration. 'He is the most infuriating man alive.'

The girl grinned at her, showing no sympathy at all. 'If you say so, miss.'

'And, I think I may be in love with him.' It made

her feel a little better to say the words aloud, even in such a weak fashion. She had told herself that what she'd felt last year had been nothing more than infatuation. She had wanted to keep the memory of that time a secret, even from him.

When she'd met him again this Season, he had gone out of his way to charm her, and she hadn't taken that seriously, either.

But each time they met, there had been less artifice about him. Then, yesterday, she'd been moved as he'd spoken about himself. And in the evening, she was far too angry at the thought that he might take a mistress.

Today, when she'd planned to break from him…

She looked at the Bible, sitting in her lap, a book she'd assumed was lost forever. But he had known she would be missing it and kept it for her.

She looked at Bessie, again. 'He cares about me. More than the other men I have met, at least. And when I am with him? I feel…' She struggled to find words. 'I feel. Just that. Sometimes, he makes me angry, or frustrated. But with others, I mostly feel nothing at all.' She gave the maid a hopeful look. 'Is that love?'

'I could not say, miss,' she replied. But she was smiling as if she wanted to say yes. Then, her smile disappeared as she looked towards the exit. 'Oh, dear.'

Cassie turned to see Portia, hurrying down the path towards them. 'There you are.'

'It seemed like a nice day for a walk.'

'Alone?' Portia said with a sceptical smile.

Cassie spread her hands gesturing to the lack of companions.

'At least you have brought your maid with you. It is never wise to meet a gentleman without a chaperone.'

'What gentleman?' Cassie said, looking around her.

'You know perfectly well it was Westbridge. He was leaving the park just as I entered, and he looked happy.'

'Is that really so strange?' Cassie said.

'Very,' Portia said, frowning. 'I have never seen him happy.'

'Do not be ridiculous. He is always smiling,' Cassie replied.

'Smiling? Yes. Boisterous. Jovial. Ebullient. Always in the highest spirits and with the quickest wit. But he is never simply, sincerely, content.' Portia's eyes narrowed. 'How long has this been going on?'

As Cassie prepared another denial, Portia cut her off.

'And do not tell me there is nothing. I am not as blind as Julian is. You look at him differently than you do your other suitors.'

'How?' she said, honestly curious.

'As if you are listening to what he is saying,' Portia said with an exasperated huff.

She could not deny it. So she shrugged and smiled. And she felt a strange sense of relief.

'How well do you know him?' Portia said and gave her the sort of penetrating look that would be very hard to lie to.

Where should she begin? With the ball? With the duel?

'Your hesitation is making me anxious,' Portia said, probably assuming the worst.

'After the duel, I was afraid Julian would be charged with murder. I went to the Duke's house and nursed him.'

'How noble,' Portia said with a grim expression. 'But that is not what I mean. How well do you *know* him?'

Cassie blushed. 'A few kisses.' She thought. 'Two. Only two.' Somehow, it had seemed like more.

Portia's eyebrows rose. 'Interesting.'

In what way, Cassie wondered. Was that too many? Too few? 'He gave me this,' Cassie said, holding up the Bible in defense. Then, she added,

'I left it in his bedroom,' which quite spoiled the explanation.

Portia stared at her for a moment, stunned to silence. Then, she shook her head and held up a hand in defeat. 'This will make an interesting story which you can tell me at a later date. The immediate question is what you are planning to tell your brother.'

'Me?' The word came out as a squeak.

'You,' Portia said in a firm voice.

At first, she had thought that there would be a way to hide the truth indefinitely. But things were changing. If the Duke was serious in pursuing her, at some point, everyone would learn of it.

'The longer you wait, the more difficult it will become,' Portia said in a stern voice. 'And I have no intention of helping you.'

'I didn't expect you would,' Cassie assured her. 'But, perhaps, Westbridge...'

Portia let out a sharp laugh. 'That would be...' She shook her head. 'Inadvisable.'

'The man is normally the one to go to the family.'

'If they are serious about the future,' Portia said, giving her another serious look.

Was he serious? She still did not know. 'He made an offer,' she said, grasping at the bit of good news.

'Of what?' Portia said, with a doubtful smile.

'Formal wedding, with banns read and all.'

Portia's look of surprise returned, and for a moment, she was quiet, as though thinking. 'It still must come from you. The relationship between the two men is cordial now, but it has been volatile. We do not want them to come to blows over a misunderstanding.'

Cassie nodded. She could not say that she liked the idea of talking to Julian, but she could see the truth in what his wife was saying. If she was serious in her feelings about the Duke, she would need to negotiate a safe path forward for all of them.

Portia's smile relaxed, and she held out a hand. 'Come. We will go home together, as if nothing has happened. Supper will be late tonight as Parliament is in session. You will have time to think of what to say to Septon, when he comes home.'

Cassie rose and gestured to Bessie and they walked to the entrance of the park where a carriage was waiting to take them back to the townhouse. Once there, she went to her room and pretended to nap before supper. But sleep was impossible with her mind racing over the things she needed to say when she came to the table.

When Julian finally arrived and they sat down to eat, she refilled her wine glass three times. But by the time that dessert was served, she'd said nothing of importance, limiting herself to smiles and nods and agreeing with her brother's opinion about the quality of the food and the disappointing state of English politics.

When her brother got up to leave, Portia announced, 'I think Cassandra has something she wishes to say.'

He turned back to her, smiled and waited.

This was the moment. She said a silent prayer for strength, opened her mouth and said, 'I just wanted to thank you again for this wonderful opportunity. I am enjoying my time in London very much.' Then, she fell silent again, ignoring Portia's frustrated sigh.

Julian looked at her, confused. Then, he said, 'You're welcome. And now, I think it is time for me to retire.'

'Good night,' she said with a nervous smile.

And then, he was gone. Portia followed him after one final annoyed look in her direction.

Cassie's hand shook as she raised her glass and drained the last of her wine. This was not a failure, she told herself. Only a delay. Nothing bad had happened, as of yet. She still had time to work this out. She would take the night to think it out.

Tomorrow, she would explain everything.

Chapter Thirteen

The next day, Sebastian was taking his usual morning coffee at White's, and feeling exceptionally pleased with himself. Last night's session in the House of Lords had been productive. There had been very little wrangling on several important votes and all had gone as he'd hoped.

It had been the finish of a wonderful day.

Not a perfect one. He had gone home to sleep alone. But his dreams had been of Cassie, and what it might be like to meet her over the dinner table, after a night of politics. In his sleep, he'd offered her a kiss on the cheek, basked in her smiles, as she took her seat beside him. She had been wearing a white gown, the amber pin glittering on her left breast, and staring at him with a devoted smile. After a pudding of apricots and cream, he had suggested that they retire, and she'd followed him up the stairs to his room.

And then, the dream had ended, just when it should have been getting interesting. Strangely, he had not minded. While there was a lot to be said for lurid, erotic fantasies, the women in them never stayed to breakfast. They might declare him a god in the bedroom, but evaporated like smoke before making him feel whole, or real or good.

The idea that he could have both a lover and a friend was a novelty. He had known from the first moment he'd seen her that he had wanted Cassie to share his bed. When he'd recognized her love, it seemed only natural that they should marry. But only lately had they begun to talk, and he wanted more of it. Their chats were rarely private and far too short.

If they could have a proper courtship, innocent conversation would be encouraged. But they could only have that with Septon's permission. Technically, his sister was of age and could make her own decisions. But that did not mean that Julian could not make the way forward difficult. If he withdrew his financial support, she might have to leave London. Or, he could do as Sebastian had done to Blake and encourage her to travel somewhere that he would never think of looking for her.

There was also the fact that Cassie loved her brother and would not want to cross him by choosing a husband he did not like. This was probably the reason she was so reticent to admit how they'd met. But if she accepted him, the next time he offered, he did not want her to have to choose between the two of them. He had to negotiate a truce with Septon.

Since Julian had just entered the room and was coming towards him, now might be a good time to practice his diplomacy. He smiled and gestured to the chair beside him. 'Good morning, Septon.'

His friend signalled a waiter to bring his tea and took his usual seat. Then, he gave Sebastian a curious look. 'You are in an exceptionally good mood this morning.'

'Indeed,' he said, still smiling. 'I slept well.'

'With whom?' Julian said with a sly smile.

'Alone,' he replied, setting his coffee aside.

Now Julian stared in amazement. 'That was not what I was expecting to hear.'

'People change,' he said with a shrug. 'You are not the man you were a year ago.'

'Because I married,' Julian agreed.

'So you have not been there to notice my absence at any of our old haunts,' Sebastian said.

Julian laughed. 'I cannot believe it.' It was an annoying reaction, but not unexpected.

Sebastian kept his expression and tone neutral, as if it did not matter to him. 'It is harder to prove a negative than a positive. When I go to bed alone, taking someone to witness and report the truth rather defeats the point.'

Septon sipped his tea. 'I suppose that is true.'

'And is marriage still everything you hoped for?' Sebastian prompted. 'Because, I was thinking I might...'

Before he could finish this, a shadow fell across the two of them and he looked up to see Gerald Balard standing nervously in front of them. As usual, Balard was perfectly pressed and band box fresh.

Sebastian reached for his coffee again and pretended that his grimace was due to the bitterness of the beans and not the overwhelming loathing he felt for the man.

Without waiting for an invitation, Balard took the third chair in their little group and glanced from one of them to the other. Then, he signalled the waiter and asked for a cup of tea.

It was far from an unusual request. But it was the same beverage that Septon was drinking. The fact seemed significant.

He looked hopefully in Julian's direction.

Julian drank again and looked over his cup at the interloper. 'Good morning, Balard.'

'Good morning, Your Grace,' he said. 'I just

wanted to tell you how much I enjoyed sharing your box at the theatre the other night.'

'There was space,' Julian said. 'I saw no reason why you could not share it.'

It was not a particularly enthusiastic response, and a little of Balard's cheerfulness seemed to drain away. Then he rallied. 'It was kind, all the same. I enjoyed Miss Fisk's company, as well.'

'I see.' Julian went back to his tea, not making it any easier on the fellow. Though his smile was not obvious, Sebastian knew him well and could see the very faint curve in his lips as the silence stretched to awkwardness. Then he looked directly at Balard and said, 'Was there something else you wished to say?'

'Yes, Your Grace.' Balard squirmed in his chair, reached for his tea and spilled a bit into the saucer, then set it down again.

'You had best be about it, then,' Julian said.

'It is about Miss Fisk,' he said, and took a deep breath. 'I mean to propose to her tonight, at the Fallon ball.' Then he added, 'With your permission, of course.'

Sebastian took another sip of his coffee, staring down into the dregs and wishing he was not forced to witness this conversation he should have no part in. God, how he hated Balard. He hated every last neatly trimmed hair on his head, and each overly white tooth in his broad, innocent smile. He was rich and good-looking and earnest. And as flavourless as unripe cheese.

What he hated most of all was that there was no reason for Septon to refuse him. He would be an ideal husband for someone's sister. Inoffensive. Neutered. No threat at all.

Julian knew it as well and could not resist toying with him. 'To discuss it here is rather unconventional,' he said, giving the fellow a sidelong look.

'I could not wait a moment longer,' Balard admitted. 'The other night was delightful. I have not stopped thinking of it since.'

'The evening was delightful?' Julian said, raising his eyebrow.

'And Cassandra was, as well.'

Julian frowned.

'I mean, Miss Fisk,' Balard corrected.

Julian paused again, allowing the tension to build. Then, he said, 'Well, you will have no objection from me.'

Balard exhaled his held breath. 'That is good to know.'

'The matter is between you and my sister,' Julian reminded him.

Sebastian stared into his empty cup. It was too soon. Far too soon. He had just begun to make headway with Cassie, only to have another man step in front of him. Balard was the sensible choice and she was a sensible girl.

'I think I can handle Cassandra,' said Balard with another earnest grin.

The disgusting display of self-confidence annoyed Sebastian all the more. It sounded as if he meant to brush any objections aside.

Even Julian seemed dubious. He gave Balard another thoughtful look. 'When the moment comes, do not mention horses.'

'No horses,' Balard said, with an obedient nod.

Horses? Why would a man who had the undivided attention of Cassandra Fisk want to waste precious time talking of that?

'If that is all?' Julian gave Balard an expectant look.

'Of course, Your Grace,' he said with a bob of his head. 'Thank you so much for sparing the time.'

'Good luck,' Julian added, then went back to his tea. Once the man was gone, he set the cup aside and called for the waiter, 'Brandy.' He glanced at Sebastian, then said, 'Two.'

Sebastian looked at his watch. 'It is before noon.'

Julian laughed. 'When has that ever mattered to you? Besides, we have reason to celebrate.'

One of them did, perhaps. But at this point, there

was little he could do but play along. So, he accepted the drink and offered his thanks.

Julian smiled and took a reverent sip. 'Glad to have that over with.'

'What?' Sebastian said, trying to focus on his friend.

'The matter of Cassandra,' Julian said. 'Getting her launched and hitched.'

'You think that is your job, do you?' Sebastian said.

'As head of her family? It rather is.' Julian frowned for a moment. 'My father did not do right by her. I needed to make up for those years of neglect. Getting her married to the right sort of man is the least I can do.'

'And Balard is that man?'

'He's the best so far.' Julian took another sip. 'Rutland was a disappointment, as you well know. And Blake?' He sighed. 'Not ideal. He has taken himself out of the running, which is just as well. But Balard?' He stared towards the door that the man had left through. 'He has promise.'

'I suppose he does,' Sebastian said. This was the moment he should offer his well wishes for the happy couple. But words had power and the last thing he wanted to do was to hex his own chances by supporting his adversary.

He said nothing more about it and tossed off the last of his drink. Then, he stood up and smiled down at Julian. 'I must be off. I have an appointment this afternoon and must not be late.'

'Will we see you tonight at the Fallon ball?'

'I have not thought that far ahead,' Sebastian said.

'You never do,' Julian said, shaking his head as if he knew.

He did not know.

He would have been exceptionally surprised to find that Sebastian went no farther than the reading room where he scribbled out two letters, sealed them up and handed them to a footman with instructions for delivery and a generous stipend to be sure his orders were followed.

Then, he left the club to set the rest of his plan in motion.

Cassie had just finished writing a letter to her mother when the note arrived. The outside was blank with no indication that it was meant for her and the seal on the back was blank, as well. But the maid who handed it to her said the footman who'd brought it had made her swear that it would come to Cassandra Fisk and no one else.

'Thank you,' Cassie said, waiting until the girl left before popping the wax and unfolding it.

Meet me at one on Hyde Park Corner. Come alone.

There was no signature.

She should not be surprised. Nothing she'd received from him so far had been signed. She had no doubt he was the sender of this. And now he had summoned her.

She closed her eyes and smiled. It was not a love letter. Why did it make her feel as if he had whispered those few words in her ear? Her skin tingled. Her heart beat faster. And deep inside her, something strange and indescribable was happening, as if someone had opened a door that she had not known existed.

What he was suggesting was simply not done. She should throw the letter in the fire and berate him at the ball tonight for even suggesting it.

Instead, she went up to her room and rang for Bessie, so she could change into a walking dress. Then, she said. 'I am going out. You are staying here. If anyone should ask for me, you will tell them that I am napping and do not wish to be disturbed until it is time to dress for the ball.'

The girl looked surprised for a moment, then nodded. 'Very good, miss.'

Then, after pinning the stick pin to her dress, she hurried down the stairs and out the door.

As she walked to Hyde Park, she could not help imagining what Sebastian meant by his message. He had not suggested she pack anything. He was not planning an elopement. It was foolish of her to be thinking of such a thing. But perhaps he meant to offer again, as he had last week on the street.

It had to be something of a personal nature, else why would he have told her to come without a maid? Of course, there were many things that a wicked man might attempt when no chaperone was present. She had only to think about Andrew Rutland to know that.

Her steps slowed. Sebastian Morehead was not like Rutland. He was far worse. He had never denied that he was a rake. The fact that he had not tried anything inappropriate lately was not a reason to trust him or assume that he meant anything honourable by luring her out of the house unchaperoned.

Even if his intentions were good and he meant to marry her, how would she hold his interest? He was used to the likes of Harriette Wilson and the Duchess of Ashton. There was nothing so very special about her. He would be bored with her before the honeymoon was over.

She stopped.

She should go home immediately.

She turned back, staring at the way she had come.

Then, slowly, she turned towards Hyde Park. She walked, her pace growing faster with each step. Perhaps the Duke was wicked. Perhaps he was not. She knew only one thing with surety: she loved him. Whatever happened today, it was something that she wanted, for herself.

That made it different from many of the other things that had happened since she'd been in London. Julian might love her dearly, but he was trying to make her fit like a piece into a puzzle that he'd made without consulting her. From now on, she would make her own decisions, and let the results tell her if she had been right or wrong.

She was out of breath when she reached Hyde Park Corner. Only then did she realize that she'd run the last few blocks in her eagerness to learn what was going to happen. She stood, looking around her, not sure what she was expecting to see. She was not alone. Walkers passed her from all directions, coming and going from the park. But none of them seemed to take a particular notice of her.

Then, a carriage pulled forward from the place it had been parked and the door was pushed open. A man's hand extended towards her.

Without looking, she reached for it and was pulled inside and onto a seat.

The Duke shut the door behind her and smiled as they pulled forward and out into traffic.

'You wished to see me, Your Grace,' she said. He sat across from her, looking handsome and dapper as always, not flushed and breathless as she was.

'I think, under the circumstances, you should call me Sebastian,' he said.

'And just what are the circumstances?' she said, before adding, 'Sebastian,' enjoying the delicious way the name felt on her tongue.

'I am kidnapping you,' he replied, still smiling, then added, 'Cassandra. Or do you prefer that I call you Cassie?'

'Either will do,' she said, trying to control the fluttering feeling inside her so she could banter as they usually did. 'And is it really a kidnapping, if I came willingly?'

His smile faded, but only a little. 'Willingly at first. But I expect, very soon, you will have second thoughts and be quite angry with me. You will demand that I take you back to your brother's house. When you do, I will refuse.'

This sounded a bit ominous, but not really frightening. 'Where are you taking me?' she said, hoping the answer would help her decide.

'To some rooms I keep in Soho, where I entertain especially close friends.'

'Female friends, I suppose,' she said, giving him a cynical smile.

'You understand the situation perfectly,' he said.

'Do you mean to seduce me?' It was surprising that her voice did not shake. Her insides felt like a swarm of fluttering moths.

He tipped his head to the side and gazed up at the roof of the coach, considering. 'That depends. I wish to talk to you where we can be alone. We need to settle some things between us. What happens after that?' He looked down at her and shrugged. 'We will decide when the time comes.'

This sounded positively reasonable. She was not in any danger, as of yet, and he made it sound as if she would have some say in whatever proceeded. She probably should not be orchestrating her own ruin. But it was better than what might have happened had Mr Rutland continued to pursue her. For now, she would smile and wait.

A short time later, the carriage drew to a stop, and Sebastian leapt to open the door and help her down.

She hesitated for only a moment before taking his hand and letting him lead her towards a nondescript building. He unlocked the front door and urged her up a short flight of steps to a landing with another locked door. He fumbled with the key for only a moment. Then he let her into a darkened sitting room.

It took a moment for her eyes to adjust to the dim light and realize that they were not alone.

Harriette Wilson was sitting on a velvet chaise on the other side of the room.

Chapter Fourteen

She turned around to go back down the stairs, nearly pushing Sebastian down before he could stop her. 'Take me back to my brother's house this instant.'

'I told you you would say that,' he said pushing her gently back until they were both inside the room and he could shut the door. Then he locked it and dropped the key in his pocket.

'I don't know what you have in mind,' she said looking between him and the courtesan, 'but if it is what I suspect, I would rather die.'

He gave a suggestive waggle of his eyebrows, 'Why, Miss Fisk, what a lurid imagination you have.'

She glared at him and folded her arms, waiting for an explanation.

'I brought Harriette here to bear witness to my character. I could not exactly arrange a meeting between the two of you anywhere you might be seen. Hence this visit to my *pied-à-terre*.'

Cassie bit her lip to keep from speaking. She had been tempted to announce that his character must be bad indeed if he chose a whore to vouch for him. But even though the woman sitting in front of her was infamous, it seemed rather impolite to call attention to the fact.

Sebastian smiled and said, 'Harriette, may I present Miss Cassandra Fisk?'

'Septon's charming sister,' the other woman said with a smile. 'I am pleased to meet you, my dear.'

'Miss Wilson,' she said, trying to keep the chill from her voice.

'Harriette, could you tell Miss Fisk what we were speaking of at the theatre two nights ago?'

Her mouth formed an O of understanding, which relaxed into a smile. 'So this is…'

Sebastian nodded.

'I see.'

'I do not,' Cassie said, frowning.

Harriette nodded. 'I noticed that Westbridge was alone in his box and offered him company.'

'While watching the play?' Cassie said, still frowning.

'And after,' Harriette replied.

'Now, Miss Wilson,' Sebastian said, like a barrister questioning a witness, 'Before that evening, when was the last time we were together?'

'About a year and a half ago,' the woman replied.

'And, if you were to write your memoirs, how much space would you allot to me? A chapter? A page perhaps?'

The woman's smile turned catlike. 'A footnote.'

Sebastian winced. 'Let us say a paragraph, for the sake of my pride.'

'If you wish,' she replied.

'And on the night in question, how did I answer your offer of company?'

'You said that your heart was engaged, and turned me down,' she said. She was still smiling, but now it was at Cassie.

For a moment, the room had seemed to shift beneath her, and she had felt quite weak.

Then, Sebastian's hand was on her shoulder, guiding her to a chair and pushing down until she sat. Once she was settled, he turned back to Harriette. 'And before that evening, you had not seen me in some time?'

'A year and a half,' she repeated.

'Have you heard anything else about me, recently?'

'Only that people were wondering what you were

up to,' she replied. 'No one has seen you in your usual haunts in ages.'

'No gambling? No whoring? No drinking late into the night?'

'Not that I am aware of,' the courtesan said. 'Since the duel with Septon, the gossip about you is that there is no gossip.'

'That will be all, Miss Wilson,' he said, bowing deeply to her and indicating the door.

'Then I shall just leave the two of you alone, shall I?' she said, smiling brightly. 'Unless you need a chaperone?'

He cleared his throat and gave a slight shake of his head.

'Very well,' she said and looked to Cassie. 'You needn't worry that I will speak to you, should we meet again, Miss Fisk. As far as the *ton* is concerned, we have never met.'

Then, before she could decide whether to offer thanks or objections, Sebastian had unlocked the door and let Miss Wilson out into the hall. He shut the door again, and they were alone.

He did not lock it again, instead going to the front window and moving the curtain, peering down into the street to watch Miss Wilson's departure.

Cassie glanced at the exit, only a few feet away. If she wished, she could be out the door and down the stairs before he could do anything to stop her. Once outside, she would have to flag down a hackney and hurry home before anyone had missed her.

She looked back at the Duke. *Sebastian*, she thought, and could not resist a small smile. She had made her decision about him before she'd arrived at Hyde Park. She would not run away now.

He turned back to her and smiled. 'May I offer you refreshment? Tea? Lemonade? There is a tray made up in the pantry. Or perhaps, something stronger.'

'I thought you said the apartment was unoccupied,' she said, furrowing her brow. 'You seem rather well-prepared.'

'I have a woman who keeps it clean and ready, should I need it without warning,' he said. 'I wrote to her that I would be entertaining this afternoon.' He paused. 'She is long gone, by the way. We are all alone.'

'How convenient,' she said, watching him. Then, she glanced around, examining her surroundings. If this was a den of sin, it did not disappoint. The walls were enamelled a dark green, and the furniture consisted of several couches in leather and velvet, accompanied by small tables just right for a glass of wine or a plate of hors d'oeuvres to nourish lounging lovers. On the wall above the fireplace there was a gold-framed print of a naked woman, climbing into a bath.

'Who is that?' she said, pointing to the woman in the drawing.

'It is supposed to be the Prince Regent's mistress,' he said. 'But I do not think it looks very much like her.'

'I hope you are talking about her face,' she said, giving him a dubious look.

He laughed. 'Yes. Her face. But I will say, the rest of her is attractive enough to attract a king.'

She stared at the picture, again. 'I have no opinion on that.'

'Well, I am something of a connoisseur,' he said, stepping closer to admire the picture. Then, he glanced at her, as if comparing. 'There is something to be said for a woman with an air of mystery.'

She glanced down at her gown and wondered if she was dressed appropriately for the occasion. Miss Wilson had not looked as she'd imagined a Cyprian would. Her walking dress had been tasteful and expensive. Cassie felt rather dowdy in comparison. The rose-coloured spencer she wore over her muslin gown had little ornament other than the stick pin and was at least a Season old. But when she looked back to Sebastian, he was staring at her as if he could see through the wool to the skin underneath.

She resisted the urge to cover her breasts with her hand. 'There is nothing particularly mysterious about the human form. You have likely seen enough of them to know that they are all fundamentally alike.'

'And yet, all delightful in their own way,' he said, smiling. 'I once knew a courtesan with a wooden leg. It did not diminish her beauty in the slightest. A very talented woman, as well.'

She gave him a dark look.

'She played the harp,' he said, blinking innocently.

'You did not bring me here to talk about music,' she said.

'No, I did not,' he said, his smile fading into something more thoughtful. 'I brought you here because I wanted to assure you that my meeting with Harriette at the theatre was innocent. I was afraid you might have misunderstood.'

She nodded. 'You have done so. Was there anything else?'

'I have been honest,' he said, holding out his open hands. 'In exchange, I want the truth from you.'

A thrill went through her, as it always seemed to when he got too close. If she was honest, as he wanted her to be, she'd felt a strange pull at her heart the first time she'd seen him lying naked and bleeding on his bed. It had only grown, since.

He sat down on a velvet divan on the other side of the room, looking across at her and his smile vanished. 'I have thought of nothing but you for months now. I cannot eat. I cannot sleep.'

She snorted. 'You look both well-rested and well-nourished to my eyes.'

He shrugged. 'An exaggeration, perhaps.'

'And you wonder why I have trouble trusting you,' she said, shaking her head. 'You cannot go two minutes without telling a lie.'

'Well, this, at least, is God's truth. I have not lain with a woman since before the duel.'

She could not help her start of surprise. She looked into his eyes, searching for any sign that he was lying again.

But his expression was as earnest as she'd ever seen it and he did not look away. 'Until I found you again… Until I had spoken to you and learned if I had any reason to hope? I could not think of bedding another.'

'I suppose this is meant to impress me,' she said with a nervous laugh.

'I am only stating what happened,' he said, still staring at her.

She was impressed. At least a little. Wasn't this just what she'd dreamed of? A man so changed by a single kiss that he could devote himself to her for the rest of his life?

She shook her head, rejecting the idea. When she'd found him, he'd been too weak to fight for his own life without her help. Now he expected her to believe that he had the strength for celibacy.

'I have curtailed my late nights, as well,' he added. 'I still drink and gamble, of course. I am not some starched-up prig who means to lord his virtue over others. But I do not partake of anything enough to call it a vice.' He held out his hands again, as if to show he was open and honest. 'I had given up hope that I could be the man my title deserved. I was close to death. Then, I met someone who changed all that. Tell me. Are you that woman?'

A happy warmth flowed to every part of her, enveloping her like a hug. She stared into his eyes which, as always, were blue and clear. They'd been so when he was wicked and were no indication of a pure heart. But they could see through her lies, easily enough and she was tired of denying him.

She nodded. 'I have not told Julian how we met,' she said.

'I did not think you would,' he replied.

'I thought, perhaps you would not remember me,' she added.

'As I said, I could not forget.'

'And when you did? I thought your interest was just a trick to lure me into your bed,' she whispered.

'Not a trick,' he said, smiling. 'I want that, of course. But so much more.'

'But I am not afraid anymore. I was the one who nursed you,' she said, feeling a flood of relief along with the truth.

'You were the one I kissed,' he said more softly.

'And then, I left you,' she reminded him. 'What choice did I have?'

'You could have stayed,' he said.

'As your mistress?'

This gave him pause, which was proof, she supposed that that was what he'd wanted at the time.

'My brother had hopes for me,' she said. 'More than I had for myself. I did not want or need a husband. But I did not wish to disappoint him. And my father…'

'The vicar?' he said with a sad smile.

'He would never have understood. They would have blamed you for a situation that was not your fault. You would have been forced to marry me.'

'And you did not want that?' he said, his expression open but curious.

'We had just met,' she said. 'You were still weak from an injury my brother had caused. You could not possibly…' But there was something about the way he was looking at her that made her stop. He had proposed in the street. Repeatedly. He had forsworn other women while he searched for her. 'It was all very complicated,' she finished.

He said nothing now, waiting for her.

'It still is,' she said, nervous.

'Not really,' he replied and patted a place on the couch next to him. 'If you come here, I will show you how easy it can be. And how pleasant.'

He was right. It would be easy. Even easier, if she had the strength to stand. Just looking at him, her knees turned to water. 'On the couch,' she said. The piece of furniture he had chosen did not look like it was designed for sitting and taking tea. But it would be perfect to recline on if one was pushed onto one's back and…

Now she felt dizzy.

'I could have suggested the bedroom,' he said, his roguish smile returning. 'But its decoration would probably shock you.' His lips quirked. 'In fact, I am sure it shall. It is not the sort of thing a vicar's daughter should see.'

'I have been in your bedroom before,' she said, gathering her strength.

'In my home,' he said. 'That is quite different.'

What on earth was she doing? She should demand

to be taken home and insist on a proper courtship, if he was serious in pursuing her. But if he meant to marry her as he'd claimed a week ago, what would happen was inevitable. All roads led to the same place.

But some of them were more interesting than others.

'I think I should like to see it,' she said and rose from her seat.

He suppressed a chuckle. 'You continue to amaze me, Miss Fisk. And I do like to be surprised.' He walked across the room and stood behind her. 'Very well, then. Let us begin your education.' He wrapped his arms around her and covered her eyes. Then, he steered her forward towards what she guessed must be the bedroom door.

Chapter Fifteen

She allowed him to guide her, leaning back against him and enjoying the decadent feel of his body pressing against her back. He was solid and warm, and he smelled of oranges and cloves and a hint of bay.

They stopped and his hands dropped to her shoulders.

Her eyes had been closed behind his fingers. Now she opened them and looked around.

The walls were green as the sitting room had been, but the enamel had been replaced by coverings of padded baize, attached to the plaster with brass studs.

'It is an exceptionally quiet room because of the hangings,' he said.

She stared at the satin-covered bed which dominated the room. 'I suspect it is good for sleeping.'

'And other things,' he agreed. 'You can scream

all you want here and no one on the street will ever know.'

'Am I likely to?' she said, her nervousness returning.

'We shall see,' he replied, then said, 'Look up.'

She laughed. She could not help it. The entire ceiling was covered with a mural, nymphs and satyrs engaged in acts of unrestrained debauchery around a gathering of cherubs that framed a mirror above the bed. 'Did you…' she choked.

'It was this way when I rented the place,' he replied. 'But I will admit, its presence was a deciding factor in my signing the lease.' Then, his right hand slid off her shoulder to cup her breast.

She froze for a moment, shocked. Then leaned back again and relaxed into his touch. What was the point of being seduced by a rake if it was some mundane deflowering on a white cotton sheet with the lights extinguished? If she was going to fall from grace she wanted to land with a crash.

A crash that would not be heard outside of this room, at least.

'You are wearing the pin I gave you,' he said, against her ear. 'I like it when you do that. It excites me.' His other hand undid a button on her spencer.

'An ant excites you,' she said, trying to work out

the logistics in a joining of two, or was it three, mythological creatures in the painting above her.

'It has been a year,' he said, undoing the rest of the buttons. 'At this point, nearly everything excites me.' He released her long enough to pull the jacket from her shoulders and placed it on a chair. Then, he stood behind her again and returned to his fondling while he nibbled her neck. His right hand slid lower to her belly, pressing their hips together.

'Oh my,' she said as a particularly well-endowed satyr leered down at her from the ceiling.

'If you see anything that interests you?' He bit her shoulder. 'Just let me know.'

'I couldn't begin…' she said, shaking her head. There was nothing familiar in the painting above her. Every one of them made her feel confused and strange. Not bad, precisely. But definitely different than she'd felt before seeing them.

'Then I shall be your sommelier,' he said. 'I will offer pleasures. You may take them or leave them, as you see fit.' He reached between them and undid the fastenings at the back of her gown, pushing it off her shoulders and letting it fall to the floor. Then, he took her hand and let her step out of it before taking it and hanging it on a peg in the wardrobe so it would not wrinkle.

She was still wearing a bonnet and gloves, and

her shoes, which seemed very silly given the circumstances. So she dispensed with them, arranging them as neatly as he had the rest of her clothing.

He was being very careful. She had imagined that, with a rake, there would be more rending of garments. Of course, she usually imagined that there would be more resisting on the part of the girl involved. She should not judge.

He returned and stood in front of her, glanced down at her body and smiled. Then, he looked back up into her face, touching her cheek with his hand. 'When I look into your eyes, I am undone.' He lowered his mouth to cover hers and she opened to his kiss.

It was different than it had been the last time. A year ago, he'd been playful, teasing her into responding before she'd known what was happening. But this kiss began slow with the barest touch of his tongue, as if it was his first. The thought made her smile. He felt the change and responded to it, moving against her, sipping and nipping, tasting and savoring.

She kissed him back, just as carefully, her tongue sliding against his and into his mouth. The feeling was safe and exciting all at once, as if the fragile barriers between them were fading away. She gave a hazy thought to the pictures above them, and the very real joining that was to come. The pleasure of the kiss was sweet and delicious. But it was not enough. She wanted more.

The gentle exploration grew to something more demanding. He pressed a hand to the back of her neck, urging her on until she was licking into him and nibbling his lips, dizzy with the need to know him.

His hands moved down her back to the ties of her petticoat and the laces of her stays, stripping her, pushing them out of the way until she stood in shift and stockings, her arms wrapped around his neck, rubbing her nearly naked body against him.

Then, he pulled away, in a flurry of breathless bites on her swollen lips. 'I am wearing far too much clothing. Let us take care of that, shall we?' He lifted her hands to the knot of his cravat and went to work on the buttons of his waistcoat, peeling off his coat and throwing it aside with none of the gentleness he'd used on her garments.

She rushed as well, pulling at knots, tugging his shirt free of his breeches and drawing it up and over his head, then arching her back as he seized her by the waist and buried his face in her breasts. He tugged the shift down and grazed her nipples with his teeth before taking them, one after the other, into his mouth with long, greedy pulls. Desire flowed in her like blood, rushing to the places he kissed and down again to pool between her legs, leaving her wet and wanting.

As if from a great distance, she heard herself making small, needy noises, pleading for things she did not know she wanted.

He answered with a growl and walked back with her towards the bed, pushing her down on it as he hurried to strip away the last of his clothes. Then, he was on the mattress with her, pushing her legs apart and burying his face between them. As his hands undid her garters and smoothed her stockings down her legs, his mouth was doing unspeakable things to her body, kissing places she had never thought a man could kiss.

She stared up at the ceiling and saw her own reflection in the mirror and the knowing smiles of the cherubs as he took her, his tongue darting into her before his teeth found a place that made every muscle in her body jump. His hands slid back up her thighs and his fingers were on her, then in her, moving in time to the thrust of his tongue.

The pressure grew. And suddenly, she knew why he'd talked of screaming. She was making sounds she'd never heard before as he took her, played with her, ravished her. The woman she could see in the mirror, naked and writhing in ecstasy, one hand on her lover's neck and the other playing with her own breasts, was as wanton as any of the nymphs on the ceiling.

Suddenly, it was all too much. She was sure, if this did not end immediately, she would shatter like glass. But before she could tell him to stop, the change she was fearing happened and it was not her that broke, it was whatever bonds had tethered her to the earth. She was free for the first time in her life, flying, floating, drifting back to earth as light as a feather in a breeze.

She could feel Sebastian stroking her hip, murmuring endearments against the inside of her thigh. Then, she felt him move, sliding up, stretching himself to cover her body with his. 'I do not want to hurt you,' he said, stroking her hair. 'But someone will. And it must be me.'

She looked at the ceiling again, at the creatures cavorting across it and knew that, no matter how she felt now, they had just begun. Underneath the delicious sensations she had experienced, there was a deep emptiness that needed filling, and desire coiling inside her readying for another release.

She wrapped her arms around him and spread her legs, staring into the mirror at her hands stroking down his naked back to grasp his hips. 'Make me yours.'

She closed her eyes, but only for a moment. Then, she opened them and watched their reflection, and the muscles of his bum flexing as he moved. He was touching her again, stretching, shifting, nudging.

It hurt. Just as he said it would.

But they were one, and that made it better. He kissed her and let out a shaky sigh and moving very slowly, sucking his breath back through his teeth in a way that made her wonder if he hurt, as well. 'You are heaven,' he whispered. 'As I always knew you would be. An angel.'

The pain was fading. In its place, she felt a strange sense of triumph. Lust was supposed to be a sin. As were greed, avarice and sloth. She felt them all, mixed with so much sweet pleasure. If she had to deny herself these feelings, she did not want to be an angel, anymore. She wanted to be wicked.

She wrapped her legs around his and sank her fingers into his flesh, urging him on. Then, she rode the feeling as he thrust deep, surprised at how good it felt to be taken. And there were so many pictures above her. So many ways that they could join. She wanted to try them all.

She thrust up with her hips, trying to keep time with him as her muscles clenched around him and she lost herself in the feeling. Then, he was faltering, shuddering, crying out as he said she might, and finally, collapsing on top of her, spent.

They rested for a time, and then he kissed her light and playful, his body still a part of her. Then, he smiled at her, eyes sparkling and said, 'Tell me, sweet. How do you like being a fallen woman?'

Chapter Sixteen

Sebastian held his breath, waiting for an answer. Perhaps he should not have been so flippant over an experience as profound as this one had been. But it was easier to joke about things he did not understand, and this was unfamiliar territory for him, just as much as for her.

Though he had not done so recently, he'd made love more times than he could count. But he had never been *in love* while he'd done it. If this had been a session of a casual afternoon of prigging? He'd have known just how to behave. But he had never lain with a virgin, much less the woman he planned to marry.

He had expected there might be tears. Her eyes were not the least bit misty. But there was a lump in his throat that he had not expected. If she did not speak soon, he was going to blurt out something embarrassing that would spoil his reputation as a man of experience.

She licked her lips and he watched, fascinated. She released a theatrical sigh and said, 'If one must be ruined, I suppose this will have to do.' Then, she smiled, catlike and satisfied.

He relaxed. He had not disappointed. He rolled, pulling her after to sprawl across him.

She slid off and nestled under his arm, kissing his cheek.

'I knew, the first moment I saw you, that it would come to this,' he said, smiling back and feeling smug.

'The first moment you saw me, you were in no condition to know anything,' she said, stroking his chest. 'You were steeped to the gills in laudanum.'

'Good days,' he said. 'I did enjoy the opiates.'

'You did not seem to, at the time.' Her hand on him was as gentle as it had been that day. 'You were in a great deal of pain when I came to you.'

'Creeping into my house in the night and telling my butler that the doctor had sent you.' He patted her on the hip. 'The poor man was beside himself when he realized that he'd let a stranger come to my bedside without even asking her name.'

'I thought myself quite clever, at the time,' she replied, kissing him again. 'Julian had visited me, just as he always did on Wednesdays. And when he told me the foolish thing he'd done, I knew I had to do something to make things right.'

He smiled, flattered at her distress on his account. 'I was close to death, until you came and dragged me back from it.'

He watched in the mirror as she nodded, her hair brushing against the side of his chest. 'And what a disaster that might have been. It was bad enough that he duelled. But if he had murdered you, Julian might have been hung for murder.'

Sebastian froze, his arm around her waist. She might be snuggled close to him like a contented kitten, but she was thinking of someone else. It had been the same on the night she'd saved his life.

He had entertained himself for their year apart, trying to remember what he might have done to secure her devotion. Had he met her some night he'd been too drunk to remember? Perhaps he had forgiven the gambling debt of a male relative after ruining them at the tables. Or was she affiliated with some charity he supported? She might have seen the best of his character and decided to ignore the gossip.

None of that had been true. She had not known him or cared for him. It had been about Julian, all along. 'So you didn't come for me, after all,' he said softly.

She laughed. The sound was small and sharp as the pin he'd given her. 'I didn't know you, beyond the few times Julian had mentioned you.' She poked him in the ribs with a fingertip. 'But from what I heard, you sounded quite horrid.'

'Oh,' he said as the romantic dream he'd built around their meeting popped like a bubble. He had been remembering those days as if they were a magical holiday. But he had been near mad from pain and laudanum, stinking of blood and sweat, unable to perform the simplest tasks for himself.

He laughed, as well. It was time he came to his senses. 'I must have been a terrible patient. It is a wonder you bothered.'

'You were awful, you know. Trying to get me to read that book you had in your dresser. And the way you looked at me, as if you wanted to eat me up.' She smiled at him in the mirror and rolled her eyes. 'You were lucky that I came there to save you and not to give you what you deserved.'

He had been seeking his just deserts when he'd challenged Septon. Cassie had not been a reprieve, merely a delay of sentence. And the sweet kiss that they had shared?

He looked at the moment with clear eyes now.

'You stuck your finger in my wound to get away from me,' he said.

'You must admit, it was effective,' she said, still smiling.

He had assaulted her. She'd defended herself. But that moment was nothing, compared to what he'd done today.

How many women had he brought to this bed? How many lewd acts had he performed here? And yet, he'd brought the woman he loved to this den of iniquity, instead of carrying her over the threshold of his home after a proper wedding. He hadn't honoured her. He'd dragged her down to his level.

He must let her go immediately, before more damage was done.

He turned his head towards her so he would not see his reflection, for he could not bear to look at himself. Then, he smiled, making sure it was the false face he wore when bantering with widows and wayward wives. 'Well. This has been a very informative afternoon.'

'For both of us,' she said, giving him a lascivious smile that broke his heart.

'You have finally given me the explanation I was seeking, about last year.' He laughed again, surprised that it sounded light and natural. 'For a time,

I thought I was going mad. That I was wrong, or that you really did not remember me.'

'I had been trying to forget,' she said. 'But you made it impossible.'

Because he had stalked her, giving her no peace until she'd surrendered. What kind of monster had he become? 'Thank you for telling me the truth. And for saving me last year, of course.'

She giggled. 'You are most welcome.' She ran a hand up his chest before laying it against the side of his neck as if preparing to kiss him again. 'Your way of showing gratitude was very interesting. Would you like to demonstrate it again?'

She had been innocent when she'd come into this room, pure in a way he had very little experience with. If he'd met her before coming to London, they'd have made a match of it. But now, it was far too late.

Very carefully, he peeled her hand away, gave it a squeeze and placed it back at her side. 'Once was enough to make my point, I think.' Then he sat up and swung his legs out of the bed, turning his back on her.

She scrambled after him, sitting at his side. 'Well, then, what shall we do next?' She still sounded sweet and eager, and he hated having to hurt them both.

'We must get you back to your brother's house so

you can get ready for the ball tonight. Fallon's isn't it? I am expected there, as well.' He stood up, gathering his clothing and throwing it in a heap on the bed.

'The ball?' He could hear the awareness dawning in her voice, and the pause after the two words as she tried to find the right response. 'I thought we might go to Scotland.'

That had been his plan, as well. But if he truly loved her, he must admit that it was just as Julian had said to him. He was nothing more than an obstacle between her and the future she deserved. He had tried for a year to improve his character. But what he'd done to her today proved that he was still as awful as the day he'd met her.

She needed to be rid of him. The sooner the better.

'Scotland,' he repeated. 'I thought so too, once.' He could not look at her, so he busied himself with pouring water in the basin and going to retrieve her petticoat. 'But you refused me. Three times, in fact.'

'I did, then. But…'

He did not dare meet her eyes. If he did, he would give in and spoil the best chance she had to go forward with a man far better than himself. 'Come on, now. Have a wash, so we can get you dressed. You likely have some blood on your legs.'

The last was uncalled for, and the cruelest thing he'd ever said. But it got her moving and gave him a chance to pull on his breeches, so he did not feel quite so vulnerable. He had been unclothed in front of countless women, but he'd never felt so naked before, as if he had no defenses at all.

Once she had cleaned herself, he dropped her shift over her head and did up her stays. There was little he could do with her hair other than tie a bonnet. 'If I were you, I would not remove it until you have called your maid to set things right,' he said.

She glared at him in response. It was far less than he deserved. But at least she harbored no more illusions about his nature. It was the best outcome he could manage, given the circumstances.

'My carriage is waiting, just outside.' He checked his watch. 'It will have you home with time enough to dine and dress, so you can go out again.' He paused, for this was the hardest. 'I would not recommend that we speak with each other tonight. We would not want anyone to guess what we have done.'

'That you bedded me?' She'd been sharp with him before. But she had never sounded as cold as this. 'No. I certainly would not want anyone to suspect that.'

He gave her a satisfied sigh and ushered her to the door. 'I am glad we understand each other.'

'We do,' she said. 'Perfectly.' Then, she stepped through the door and slammed it shut.

Chapter Seventeen

She had been an idiot.

Julian had warned her to stay away from Westbridge. She had suspected from the first that those offers of marriage were hiding a darker motive. And yet, she had thrown all common sense aside and lain with him, assuming the day would end with an elopement. She deserved to be punished, for both wickedness and stupidity.

Last night, she'd been ready to tell Julian of her love for his friend. Thank God she had not. It would have made today even more complicated, when she had to announce that she'd been mistaken. The man was vile and she wanted nothing more to do with him.

At least, that's what she should have said, if she had any sense. If forced to speak of Sebastian tonight, it was far more likely that she would burst into tears and demand to know what she had done to make him turn away from her. When they'd gone into the bedroom, she had been sure that he loved her as much as she did him. But something had changed. She did not want to believe that it had been the thrill of the chase that had held his interest. Now that she was…

She bit her lip. She was not soiled, or spoiled, or any of the other horrible terms that people whispered about girls who said yes instead of no. She was still herself. A little wiser, perhaps, but not so different than she'd been this morning. If she did not fall pregnant, no one need ever know what had happened.

And if she did?

The thought hit her like a cold draft, making her shiver. Portia would know immediately who she had been with. Julian would find out. And when he learned that Sebastian had refused to marry her. There would be hell to pay. Even worse, she'd have to go back to the country and explain to her parents that, in the glamour of a London Season, she had rejected all of their teachings and turned out just like her mother.

She could not let any of that happen. If there was a child, she would not let it be cast aside and raised by strangers, as she had been. She would find a man to marry and no one would be the wiser.

But it would not be Sebastian Morehead. She

would rather die than go crawling back to him after the way he'd treated her. And if he thought she would succumb to his charms a second time, he was touched in the head. In the future, she would treat him as she had at her ball, with the same distant courtesy she'd give to a stranger. Because that was what he was: a man she did not really know at all.

She arrived home with more than enough time to have a light supper before dressing for the ball. But before she could hurry up the stairs to her room, Portia stopped her in the front hall, touching her arm.

She flinched. And in that moment, Cassie knew that she'd given it all away.

Portia stared at her, reading her guilt as if it was written in inch-high letters on her face. When she finally spoke, there was no confusion in her voice, just warning. 'Your maid said that you were in your room, napping away a megrim.'

'I decided to take a walk to clear my head.' The response was plausible. But it was a lie and they both knew it.

'I will have a light supper, sent to your room,' Portia said. 'You have plenty of time to compose yourself before we leave.' The duchess released her arm and gave her a worried smile and the faintest tip of her head to urge her up the stairs.

She did as she was told, hurried to her room and

rang for her maid. Then, she stared into the mirror, searching her face for any signs of change. There must be something, for Portia had known immediately. Something in her eyes, perhaps. The flush in her cheeks. Or was it just that, no matter how she felt now, a little while ago she had been truly happy?

It did not matter. She would spend the night hiding behind her fan, if she had to. But she would admit to nothing. Then, the maid arrived with her dinner tray. She sat down at the dressing table to eat as Bessie got a ball gown out of the wardrobe and shook the wrinkles from the skirt. She gave a sidelong look to Cassie's dishevelled hair but said nothing. By eight, she was fed, dressed and heading down the stairs to meet Portia and Julian in the hall.

Her brother gave her a smile of encouragement, taking her hands in his and looking at her as if for the first time. 'You are lovely, tonight.'

'I look as I always look,' she said, firmly. 'Save your compliments for your wife. She is wearing a new gown and is truly stunning.'

'Portia is beautiful, as well. But it is not a special night for her.'

'Nor for me,' she said, staring at him as she had into the mirror. Had he noticed something different? She did not think so.

'We shall see,' he said, giving her a knowing look.

Then he escorted them to the carriage and they were on their way.

As they travelled, Portia told her about the Fallon rose garden which was reported to be quite splendid. 'His wife, Maddie, has added a fountain at the centre,' she said. 'Evan gave her a pair of Chinese carp for their anniversary, and she felt they needed a properly splendid home.'

'You should see it by moonlight,' Julian added. 'Ask Balard to show them to you.'

'I suppose I shall,' Cassie said with no real enthusiasm. If Gerald Balard was there, it was unlikely that she would be able to avoid him. She was in no mood to socialize with anyone until she was sure she would not embarrass herself. But with Gerald chattering in her ear, she would not need to speak beyond inserting a few polite words of agreement into his monologue.

When they arrived at the Fallon home, it was as splendid as it had been described. The ballroom had doors leading out into the famous garden, which was surrounded by ivy-covered walls and lit with torches so the guests might wander through it between dances, sipping champagne and sitting on the many benches that lined the paths.

Before she could lose herself amongst the rose bushes, Gerald Balard appeared and claimed not one, but two dances, one of which was the waltz. Then, he smiled at her and said, 'It is some time before we need to stand up. Might I get you something to drink?'

She was about to refuse, for she would have preferred to stand up for a set with someone else instead of being trapped in the inevitable one-sided conversation with him. But then, from behind her, she heard the footman announce the arrival of the Duke of Westbridge.

Suddenly, a drink sounded like a wonderful idea. She smiled at Gerald. 'Could you procure me a glass of punch, please?' She normally avoided it, for it was often stronger than wine and she did not want it to go to her head. But much had changed today. If she had succumbed to one sin, then why not another?

He was gone and back in no time at all, with a tiny silver cup that was only half full.

She sipped as he talked, her mind relaxing as the punch took effect. By the taste of it, it had both madeira and champagne and probably brandy, as well. But oranges and sugar took away the sting of the liquor and it went down easily and was gone far too soon.

He noticed her empty cup and interrupted his description of the house he planned to buy, once he had married. 'Finished already?'

She held out the cup and smiled. 'I would like another, if it is not too much bother.'

'This time, I will have one as well,' he said, and went to refill her drink.

By the end of the second cup, he had finished speaking of the house and gone on to the investments that would pay for it. It was better than gossiping about other people, as he had done at the theatre.

Or horses.

But it was still not a conversation that she had any part in. She did not even have to ask leading questions to show she was interested. He ploughed onward without noticing that she had contributed nothing other than a request for a third glass of punch.

By the time she'd finished that, it was time for their waltz. He led her out onto the floor, and pulled her into his arms, smiling down at her with his very white teeth.

She smiled back, hoping she did not look as giddy as she felt. It was probably the punch improving her mood. That and the spinning. It felt like her head was floating several feet above her body.

It was a shame that Gerald was not causing this euphoria. He was a good dancer. His movements were sure. He held her gently, but firmly, and was neither too short nor too tall, so their steps matched well. He was also handsome. Gently bred. Rich. Attentive. Aside from the excessive talking, he was a very pleasant companion.

Everything about him was pleasant. But that was all. It was a shame that she felt nothing when she looked into those eyes, other than a vague sense of guilt for wasting his time.

But he did not seem bothered by her distraction, or the fact that she was ever so slightly unsteady by the end of the dance. As the music stopped, he took her arm and kept her from weaving as she walked. 'Let us go out into the garden. It is cooler there.'

Perhaps he had noticed after all, and thought the fresh air would help clear her head. 'That sounds like a wonderful idea,' she said, patting his hand. 'We must go and see the fish.'

She allowed him to lead her between banks of roses to a bench set into the edge of the white marble fountain, where their voices would be masked by the sound of splashing water. The moon was high. The air was perfumed with flowers. Music drifted from the open windows of the ballroom.

Under certain circumstances, it might have been quite romantic.

Gerald smiled at her and took her hand in his. 'Has your brother told you the reason I wished to see you tonight?'

She frowned, momentarily confused that he'd said something that required she do more than just listen. The punch must have been even stronger than she'd thought, for it took longer than it should have to come up with her answer.

'No.'

He seemed confused as well and paused before giving her a significant look. 'I spoke to him earlier today. We had tea at White's.'

'How nice for you,' she said and smiled. Her face felt funny, as if her lips were not positioned properly. She relaxed them into a frown, licked them and smiled again, hoping that she'd gotten her smile right on the second try.

She must have for he smiled back and nodded. Then he said, 'He assured me that he had no objections.'

She kept smiling as she tried to understand what he had just said. Maybe she'd lost the thread because of the fountain noise. Or perhaps this pertained to something he'd talked about in the ballroom. She really should have paid better attention. She nodded and waited for him to go on.

'He said that the decision would be up to you.' He left another, leading pause.

'How kind of him,' she said. Her brother had promised her that her life would still be her own if she came to London. If there was a choice to be made, it was no surprise that he'd let her do it for herself. She simply had to discover what the topic was. She continued to smile and waited for Gerald to give her a clue.

'So,' he said, giving her a hopeful look. 'Are we in agreement?'

There was no context in that, at all. Perhaps she should have stopped after the second cup of punch. This all might have been clearer if she was not fuddled. And he was still staring at her, waiting for an answer.

After what felt like an eternity of silence, she surrendered her pride and said, 'I'm sorry. What were we talking about?'

'Marriage, of course,' he said with an incredulous laugh.

'To you?' Inwardly, she winced. That response had been stupid as well as rude. Of course he was speaking of himself.

'We will make an excellent match,' he said, ignoring her faux pas. 'We have gotten along very well, so far.'

Probably because he would not give her space to say two words in a row. 'We barely know each other,' she said. 'The Season has just begun.'

'In a competitive situation, it is better to stake an

early claim. If one waits too long, one loses out on the best…' He stopped suddenly and waved his hand in embarrassment.

Had he been about to compare the marriage mart to a horse auction? Or was she just foxed? She had a good mind to…

She stopped as well, considering. She must be sensible about this. He meant well in offering. And hadn't she decided, just a few hours ago that a quick marriage might be necessary to cover an indiscretion? The polite thing to do would be to ask for more time. If she gave him a chance and made the effort to listen when he spoke to her, she might like him better.

She did not dislike him now. Hadn't she thought him pleasant company as they danced? He was solicitous. Honourable. Julian approved of him. Her parents would like him. And if he had a Soho flat with lurid murals and a mirror above the bed, she would never know of it because he would not dishonour her by taking her there.

That last was the punch talking. She should not have thought it. It reminded her of Sebastian and how happy she had been when she'd thought he meant to marry her. Even now, there was a sweet, sad longing in her heart for the life they might have had, if he had been the man she'd hoped he would be.

She might have sinned by being with him. Only God knew that. But if she said yes to Gerald Balard, she would make everyone happy but herself. She would be damned on earth to a future without the love she deserved.

She took a deep breath, hoping the night air would clear a little of the fog in her brain and spoke, taking care not to slur the words. 'I am sorry, Gerald. I am most flattered. But I cannot accept.'

'It was too soon,' he said, shaking his head as if the words were a scold to himself. 'I should have waited. Perhaps in a week, maybe two…'

'I don't think it will make a difference,' she said. 'I am quite sure in my feelings.'

There. She had refused without stumbling over the words or accidentally giving him hope. Now, if he would only leave, she could stay still until she was sober enough to walk back into the ballroom.

'I have breeding, family connections, everything you could want. I don't know what you expect of me,' he said, giving her a faintly disgusted look. 'You will not do better.'

Her teeth clenched behind her frozen smile. If she was not careful, she would tell him that she'd gotten three better offers last week. Each of them had been more romantic than *are we in agreement* even though they'd been delivered on a street corner and not in a moonlit garden.

Instead, she counted to ten and announced, 'Perhaps I shall not. But I would rather die a spinster than be married to you. Now please go back into the ballroom. I think I shall remain here for a while.'

Then, she gave him an owlish stare until he went away.

Chapter Eighteen

The Fallon garden was as lovely as Sebastian remembered it. He was sitting at the very back of it, in a corner where the torchlight couldn't reach. The last time he'd been here, over a year ago, he had shared this bench with the wife of an elderly earl. They'd taken turns sipping from the flask he'd brought before disappearing out a back gate to find his carriage, where they could be truly alone.

He had not seen that woman in ages. The last year of clean living had been an interesting experiment. But it was officially at an end.

If he'd found Cassie sooner, he might have saved himself the trouble of self-improvement. Once she had assured herself that her brother was safe from prosecution, she had not cared one way or the other for his health or character. She had gone contentedly back to her old life and not given him another thought.

He pulled out the same flask he'd used to woo the countess and took a long pull on it, toasted the moon and drank again. It was embarrassing to find that one was but a minor character in the most dramatic events of one's own life. But there was the truth of it. He had not been important to her.

The recent farce they'd played was even worse. He was now the villain of the piece: a despoiler of virgins. The black-hearted swine who'd seduced and abandoned her after dispensing with anyone who dared to stand in the way of his courtship. Thank God Balard had been waiting in the wings to play the hero.

If he had any sense, he was down on one knee in this very garden, making his offer. The moon was full and the stage was set. It was a damned fine night to be in love.

He took another drink and checked his watch. The waltz had been nearly an hour ago. He'd watched the beginning of the dance, which they'd shared after an hour's conversation. If his assumptions were correct, the proposal would have come after, and the happy couple would now be making the rounds of the ballroom, sharing the good news. It was an excellent time for him to catch one last glimpse of Cassie, offer her a hurried congratulation and slip away.

He dropped the flask back into his pocket and

stood up. Later, when he was home, or in Soho, or whatever dark hole he could crawl into, there would be time for more brandy. Or a woman. Perhaps two. Or maybe he could take up laudanum. It was good for numbing other pains. Why not a broken heart?

He made his way up the garden path along a bank of pink roses, ignoring the couples he passed, with their sighing and discreet handholding. He had no time for such tepid lovemaking. This afternoon, he had lain with a goddess. The rest of his life might be equally divine punishment, but he would not change a minute of the sin.

Then, he rounded a bend in the path and there, sitting by the fountain was his everything. Her white gown glowed pale in the moonlight, as did the pearls at her throat. Her face was tipped up, basking in the cool radiance as if she could soak it up like the sun.

She was alone. The damnable Balard was probably off getting the champagne so they could celebrate. If he was lucky, he could say his farewells and be off without having to shake the bastard's hand.

He squared his shoulders and walked up to her, face fixed in a polite smile and said, 'I understand congratulations are in order.'

She turned away from the moon, and stared at him with a faintly baffled expression, as if she'd forgotten his existence in the few hours they'd been apart. Her brow furrowed. 'I beg your pardon?'

She was being more polite to him than he deserved, considering the circumstances. But there was a vagueness in her expression that he did not quite understand. She was always so sharp, so focused. Could it be?

His lips twitched. She was drunk. Perhaps he was not the only one who was suffering this evening.

'Did you say something?' she said frowning.

'I offered you congratulations on your engagement,' he said, more slowly.

'We are not engaged,' she reminded him, poking him in the chest with a wavering finger.

'I am aware of that. I mean your engagement to Balard.' When she did not respond he added, 'He was going to propose, tonight.'

'What do you know about that?' Now she sounded decidedly cross.

'I was there, at White's this morning, when he spoke to your brother,' he said.

'You knew.' Her eyes narrowed. 'You knew, all along.'

'It was hardly a secret,' he said. 'The room was quite full when he petitioned your brother. Anyone could have overheard.'

She looked around her and towards the ballroom

where the majority of guests were gathered. 'So everyone knew my business but me.'

'Well, not everyone,' he said, wondering if he should have lied to reassure her. 'But it was no surprise that Balard has been courting you. A proposal was inevitable.'

'He talked to Julian, first,' she said. 'And you.'

'Not to me, precisely,' he said. 'I was there. I wrote to you immediately after.'

'To tell me?' she said, her voice slurred but sarcastic.

'To convince you to meet me,' he explained patiently. Surely, she had not forgotten the contents of his letter so soon.

'And then, you took me to your tawdry little apartment and deflowered me.' She poked him in the chest again.

He looked around them, relieved that there was no one close enough to hear her outburst. Then, he said in a hushed tone, 'That was not my plan.'

Well actually, it had been his plan. Seduction followed by elopement, topped off with a letter of apology posted to Julian from an inn in Scotland, explaining that his sister was now a duchess. But that had been when he'd thought Cassie loved him.

'And then, you sent me home,' she said, ignoring his confusion. 'Because you thought, by evening's end, I would be engaged to someone else and there would be no consequences for your actions.'

'Wait.' That had not been his intention, at all. At least, not when the day had begun. And he had not withdrawn, as he would have with any other woman. He had been so sure that they would marry, he'd been unforgivably careless. 'I didn't…'

'Ha!' Her finger poked his chest, yet again. 'Your plans have come to nothing, you…you… Despoiler of innocents!'

'Shh,' he held his hands out as if he could muffle the sound.

'I showed you,' she said, snorting. 'I refused him.'

'You… What?'

'Turned him down, flat,' she said with an emphatic nod. 'Not that it would matter to you.'

'It does…' He looked around again and finished more quietly. 'I do not want you to be embarrassed. This will be the talk of the *ton* tomorrow.'

'Then people should mind their own business,' she said, standing up and far too close to him. 'Some people, especially.' Each word was punctuated by another poke.

In the ballroom, the music stopped, and there was a smattering of polite applause. In a minute, the garden would be crowded with couples taking advantage of the intermission to enjoy the night air. He had to calm her down and end this conversation, as quickly as possible. But after what had happened between them, she needed to marry someone. 'You will feel differently about Balard in the morning. There is nothing wrong with the fellow. It would be an excellent match.'

'Then, you marry him,' she snapped. 'He is a paragon. He would likely do your character some good.'

'I am not a woman,' he said, laughing a little too loudly and grinning at a couple passing by to show them nothing strange was going on.

'And you are not ready to marry,' she said, her fists balled in anger.

'I am not.' After the mistakes he'd made with her, perhaps he never would be.

'Then why are you bothering me?'

'I…' Because, even knowing he was not worthy of her, he could not stay away. 'I shouldn't have bothered you.' He turned to go.

Before he could take a step, she grabbed his lapels and dragged him back. 'You shouldn't have bothered me?' She was shrieking so loudly that everyone must hear. He could hear the murmuring of voices as a crowd formed.

He laid a hand on her shoulder, hoping it would soothe her. 'I am sorry. Now, can we just…'

'You do not bother me,' she shouted, her hands

punching into his chest. 'I am not bothered, you philanderer. I am totally fine. You are the one who has the problem.'

'Cassandra.' He should not be calling her that. 'Miss Fisk.'

'Debaucher! Amorist!' Her fingers dug into his coat, clinging like grim death, pushing and pulling, punching and shaking, her anger uncontained.

'Cassie, please.' He pried at her hands, twisting away from her until his back was to the fountain, but she would not release him.

'Deviant!'

'What the devil is going on?' Julian pushed through the crowd that had formed around them. At the sound of his shout, her hands sprang back, releasing Sebastian just as he tried to pull away. He felt the marble ledge of the pool against the back of his knees, blocking his progress for only a moment. Then, his feet were up in the air and he was flat on his back, with a nose full of water.

He sputtered upward, pushing lily pads out of the way as his coat was grabbed again by hands far stronger than Cassie's. He was on his feet for only a moment before Julian's punch connected with his jaw, knocking him back to sprawl on the marble bench.

'Stop!' When he looked up, Portia was clinging to her husband's arm, ready to halt the next blow.

And his darling Cassie, the only woman he would ever love, had grabbed Portia, trying to pull her free and was shouting, 'Hit him again!'

Sebastian held up a hand of surrender, closed his eyes and said in the calmest tone he could manage. 'It is late. Perhaps we can continue this conversation in the morning, Septon.'

'The usual place?' his friend said, lowering his arm.

'Pistols this time, I think,' he replied. 'I did not like being stabbed very much. Let us see if a bullet wound is any better.' He smiled and pulled a wet handkerchief from his pocket, mopping at the blood on his lip.

'Very well.' Julian turned to the two women, who were now standing in silence at his side. 'I think that will be enough for the evening, Cassandra. Portia, if you would pay our respects to the hostess? I have an early morning, tomorrow.'

Then, they were gone. The crowd around him dispersed as well, turning their heads away as if it was possible to exile him from Society by ignoring him.

And he was alone, just as he deserved to be.

Chapter Nineteen

She had not thought the day could get worse.

Of course, technically, it hadn't. The long case clock in the foyer where they waited showed ten past midnight. Yesterday had been terrible. Today was a new, even more awful day. She was publicly disgraced, and still inebriated.

She'd gotten drunk and precipitated a duel almost identical to the one she'd been trying to put right a year ago. Perhaps Julian was destined to become a murderer.

Perhaps Sebastian was never supposed to live.

Portia stood beside her, cold and silent.

'Say it,' Cassie said with a sigh. 'You want to, and I deserve it.'

'I told you what would happen if you did not tell Julian the truth,' she said. She did not sound angry, so much as sad.

'I thought there would be time,' Cassie replied. It

was not much of an apology, but her head was still foggy.

'Obviously, there was not,' Portia said. 'And I do not think I will be able to talk him out of it. The scene we witnessed was damning. I don't think anyone will be able to pretend we misunderstood it.'

'At least the Duchess did not seem angry,' Cassie said with a weak smile. 'She assured me that no harm came to the fish.'

'May we all be as fortunate as the fish,' Portia said.

'I did not really want Sebastian to die,' Cassie said, in a small voice.

'I don't suppose he will offer for you.'

'I do not think so,' she replied. 'Something happened. I am not sure what.'

Portia laughed. A single, cold *ha*. 'I think it is quite obvious to everyone what happened. Now that it has, he is no longer interested in you.'

'Did you know about the proposal?' she said staring straight ahead.

'Julian told me, after we arrived here,' she replied. 'I told him it was a mistake.'

'I refused him,' she said.

'I thought you would. It is just as well. After what happened later, Mr. Balard probably thinks it a narrow escape.'

Cassie nodded, wishing she cared enough to cry over it.

The footman opened the door and Julian was there to help them into the carriage. Once they were on their way, he looked at her with disappointment and said, 'Tomorrow morning, I will hire a carriage to take you back to the Fisks. I will have need of this one to take me to my meeting with Westbridge.'

'I do not want you to fight him,' she said, staring back at him, unintimidated.

'That was not what you were saying when I punched him,' he replied.

'It was wrong when you fought him last year, and it is no better now.'

'If you had accepted Balard, he might have issued the challenge,' Julian said.

'And if you had refused him this morning, we would not be in this situation at all,' she snapped. 'I am tired of having to bear the blame of your meddling in my life.'

'I told Balard the decision was yours,' he said, surprised.

'Just as you have been telling me who you favour and who you don't, as if your opinion would make any real difference in who I loved.'

'What is there not to love about thirty thousand a year, a handsome face and a reputation as pure as snow? And what does love have to do with marriage? It is not as if Portia loved me when we married.'

'But you loved me,' his wife said with a warning smile.

'I was mad with lust for you,' he corrected. 'That is not the same thing at all. It was not until after I married you that I fell in love.' He smiled then, and for a moment, Cassie's sin was forgotten.

'Well, I feel neither love nor lust,' Cassie announced, snapping her fingers to regain his attention. 'And I do not feel either of those things directed towards me from Mr Balard. I doubt he is shedding tears at the loss of me, nor will either of us be losing any sleep.'

'All right,' Julian said, taking a deep breath to control his temper. 'Then who would you rather marry?'

A few hours ago, she'd known exactly who her husband must be. But she'd been wrong. If not Sebastian? 'No one,' she said, feeling both sad and relieved that the Season was over for her. 'Marriage does not suit me. I mean to die a spinster.'

By the look he was giving her, Julian's anger had been replaced with confusion. 'After all that I have spent on gowns and parties and the ball? It was all for naught?'

Portia interrupted. 'You are not seriously complaining about that now? At this time?' She gave him a look that, even in the dark of the carriage, seemed to sizzle in the air.

He took a breath before turning back to Cassie. 'Of course not. I do not begrudge a penny. It was meant to help you make a decision. I simply had not expected it to be that one.' He took another breath and continued cautiously, 'It just surprises me that you are giving up on marriage after so little time. I understand that you do not love the first man who offered. But perhaps there will be another.'

A week ago, she'd have agreed with him, just to keep the peace. But things had changed. *She* had changed. The thought of marrying another man while Sebastian walked the earth made her heart ache in a way she could not describe.

And then, she remembered that he could be dead by the time the sun rose.

It would not free her. She would not be a spinster. She would be a widow and grieve him until the end of her days. But there had to be something she could do to prevent the worst from happening. 'I am resolute,' she said. 'I will not marry. I will go back to the Fisks, just as you wish. People in London will forget all about me. So, really, you needn't bother with dueling over a thing that matters to no one but me.'

Julian shook his head. 'It matters to me. To Society, as well. Westbridge is a menace to all decent women. This is not his first mistake, and it is proof that he is getting worse, not better. An example must be made.'

It was probably true. If he'd used her expected engagement to cover the possible consequences of their tryst, there was no depth to which he would not sink. He could not be allowed to do it again with some other naive girl. 'You're sure you will win,' she said, swallowing unshed tears. 'Because I could not bear it if you were hurt because of me.'

'He suggested pistols,' Julian said. 'We both know he is a poor marksman. It was as close as we will come to an apology.'

'Perhaps, just a small wound, as a warning,' she suggested.

Her brother's expression was grim. 'He's already gotten a warning from me and learned nothing by it. Now he must be stopped for good.'

The carriage arrived at the Septon townhouse, and he helped her down, giving her hand a squeeze as he did so. 'Whatever happens, know that my feelings for you have not changed. You are still my sister, and I want what is best for you. Now go inside and get some sleep.' Then, he turned back to help Portia, so she did as he suggested.

* * *

Sebastian lay in the bed of his Soho flat, waiting out the hours until dawn. His wet clothes were drying on a chair by the fire and he was naked and shivering, staring at his reflection in the mirror above. Until tonight, the views provided by it had been an erotic novelty.

But he had never been alone here before. There was no beautiful woman to reassure him, and he was free to catalogue his own flaws. Tonight, stripped of clothing and confidence, he was not some invincible scion of English nobility. He was small, an insignificant thing with pale white skin and a puckered scar on one shoulder to remind him of his previous mistakes. A single prawn in the great sea of humanity and not a handsome and wealthy peer of the realm: a gift to all womankind.

He was going to die. Unlike last year, he did not particularly want to. But he deserved to. This time, the perfect woman was not going to appear at his bedside like an avatar of benediction, forgive his sins and devote her life to him. Such women came for men with a sterling character and he had no good qualities.

There was the title, of course, and all the things that attached to it. But he had always viewed that as an accident of birth. Cassandra Fisk was not the sort of woman to be impressed by a coronet.

She wanted, no, she deserved a good man. He was the antithesis of the husband God intended for her. The fact that he'd reduced her to a lascivious sot after such a short acquaintance was proof of that. She might have come to her senses and married Balard if he'd had sense of his own and stayed away from her tonight.

But he'd had to see her. And thus it would always be, as long as he lived. But in a few hours, he would meet Septon. Then, they would both be free.

One thing rankled. He could not leave her assuming that he had seduced her with the intent of abandoning her. He had done plenty of things that were wrong, but even he was not that bad.

He sat up, got out of bed and wandered through the rooms, searching cupboards and drawers, wishing that he'd made a greater effort to outfit the apartment for any use but entertaining woman. When he'd almost given up hope, he found some writing paper, a blunt quill and a half a bottle of ink in a pantry closet.

Then he sat down on one of the divans in the parlor and pulled a table close so he could write. There was just enough time to deliver a letter on his way to the dueling ground. When she awoke, it would likely be all over. But at least she would know the truth. Then, he could die in peace.

Cassie guessed the time was nearly four o'clock when she gave up trying to sleep and lit a candle off the banked coals in the bedroom fireplace. The sky was still dark. But she'd just heard the front door slam as Julian left the house to meet with Sebastian. Dawn must be an hour or so away.

She did not bother to call Bessie for help. It was hardly fair to expect the girl to go without sleep just because she could not. She stripped the nightgown over her head, washed, and dressed simply, tying her long hair out of the way.

Then, she rummaged in the jewel case for the amber ant and kissed it before pinning it to her bodice. When she'd returned from Soho, she'd taken it off and sworn she would never wear it again.

She'd not lasted a day. But it seemed proper to wear it now, a bit of mourning jewellery that would have meaning to no one but her.

She heard the sound of footsteps in the hall. They hesitated at her door. Then, a folded paper slipped beneath it and into the room, and its deliverer hurried back down the hall and away.

She frowned and rose, crossing the room to retrieve the note, unfolding and reading.

My dear Miss Fisk,

I know we once agreed to be on more intimate terms, but it hardly seems right to take the liberty, after the wrongs I have done to you.

Know that, whatever else may happen today, I am truly sorry for them. No harm will come to your brother, no matter what else may occur. I intend to delope and take whatever punishment he wishes to give to me.

But I will not lie easy in my grave if you are left thinking as you did last night that I lured you to ruin, believing that Balard would marry you and hide any accident. My intent was to charm you away from him, keeping you into the evening so the proposal would never occur.

She smiled and clutched the paper to her bosom with a relieved sigh. The truth was bad, of course. But not as bad as it could have been. She brought it down again and continued to read.

My mistake was in believing that, when you came to my house a year ago, it was out of affection for me. In the year that separated our meetings, I'd spun some wild and unlikely fantasy that you were in love with me and not just concerned for your brother's future.

I know now that it was foolish. Since I found you again, you've made it quite clear that you did not wish to renew our unusual acquaintance. It mortifies me that I continued to badger you after you made your wishes known.

As to what happened in Soho? You have nothing to berate yourself for. The fault was all mine. You were hardly the first woman to succumb to my advances there.

She gave the paper an angry shake, for that was hardly flattering.

But you were to be the last. My intention when I brought you there was to quit the apartment after that day, and share the rest of my life with you.

Her smile returned.

But then, you explained the reason that you nursed me, last year, and I realized how wrong I had been about your feelings.

He did not understand her at all. Perhaps she had not loved him at first sight. But now that she'd met with him again, she could not imagine a life without him.

I hope that what I do this morning will make up for my mistakes. To further make amends…

She had forgotten the duel. She read on, faster.

settlement…
my bank…
monies to be directed to you…

The rest did not matter.

She threw it aside, opened the bedroom door and ran down the stairs. It was not too late. It could not be. The sun was not yet up, and he and Julian would need a decent amount of light to do something as stupid as what they were planning.

She skidded to a stop in the front hall, surprised to find Banks, the butler, standing beside it as if it was normal to be at his post in what was still so close to the middle of the night.

'May I assist you, Miss Fisk?' he said, with a respectful nod.

'Has my brother gone?' she said, panting out the words.

'About ten minutes ago, miss.'

'Where? And how quickly can I get there?'

He seemed unperturbed by her desperation and answered with the same calm and measured voice he'd have used if she'd asked him about the weather.

'As for your method of transportation, I was instructed to order a post-chaise that would take you to your parents' home later in the day.' He blinked. 'It seemed wise to procure it as early as possible, in case later supply exceeded demand. It is waiting outside now.'

She waved her hands, encouraging him to speak faster. 'Wonderful. And what is the direction?'

'I am not permitted to say, miss.'

She stared at him, incredulous.

'I was ordered to tell nothing of today's location to either you or Her Grace, lest you might decide to interfere,' he said, blandly. Then, he stared at her, expectantly.

She ran back through his words, wondering what she could say that might persuade him to disobey his master.

Then, it hit her. 'Banks, where did last year's duel happen?'

'Wimbledon Common, miss. Near where they are building the windmill.'

'Thank you, Banks,' she said, throwing her arms around him. Then tried to compose herself and added, 'I should much like to see the progress on that windmill, before I go.'

'Very good, miss. I shall tell the driver.' For a moment, he seemed as if he was about to smile. But then, he looked as distant as ever. 'Your brother left money for your trip this afternoon. He did not want it to be forgotten in the rush of events. Perhaps you should take it now.' He reached into his pocket and removed a purse and opened it to reveal a thick roll of bills.

'Thank you, again,' she said, snatching it from his hand as he opened the door and walked her to the hired carriage. As she sank back into the seat, she could hear him telling the driver to take her to Wimbledon and not to spare the horses.

They took off at a trot, and she grabbed the strap above her, closed her eyes and prayed it was not too late.

Chapter Twenty

It was as good a day as any to die, Sebastian thought, staring across the field to where the sun had just crested the horizon. The first rays were shining through a mist that floated low on the dew-damp grass, and there was a faint breeze touching his face, promising a warm and pleasant morning.

The wind was against him, and the sun in his eyes, just as he wanted it. He would spare his friend no advantage, today. If Septon came to harm, even by accident, it would hurt too many others. There were rumours that, after a year of marriage, Portia was finally with child, and he should hate to see her widowed.

There was Cassie to think of, as well. But when was he ever not thinking of her?

Despite the circumstances, he smiled.

'Are you ready?' Alex Landers, his second, touched his arm and gave him a puzzled look. Landers was not so much a friend as an acquaintance with time on his hands who had never seen a duel before.

Sebastian hoped he did not disappoint.

'I am,' he said, glancing back to Julian again, then away. It was not as if he had expected his friend to bring Cassandra with him. There was no reason for a lady to witness such a grim spectacle.

Well, one perhaps. After her rough dismissal of him yesterday, he feared that she might come just to gloat. But after finishing his letter to her, he had written his banker to dispose of the unentailed part of his estate. When he was gone, she would be a very wealthy woman. If a child resulted from the most wonderful mistake he'd ever made, it could not inherit a title, but he or she would be rich enough not to care.

He smiled again, thinking of the family that might survive him. They might not miss him, but they would live well and be happy.

It was a shame that he might damage Julian's reputation with this. But he suspected that Septon would rather see him dead than married to his sister. His own rakehell ways were long behind him. Since marrying Portia, he had been an upright member of the *ton*. Society would forgive him, as they had last time he'd duelled, blaming Sebastian for everything that had gone wrong. If it came to a trial, Julian's friends in Parliament would agree that killing Sebastian was no different than putting down a mad dog: an ugly business that had to be done for the benefit of all.

Landers left him, walking to the centre of the field to meet Julian's second. Their hushed voices carried on the silent air as if they were only a few feet away. They were examining the weapons. There would be no problem. He had brought them from the apartment, and they'd been cleaned and oiled just a week ago. The powder was dry and fresh from the gunsmith.

He was surprised that he felt no fear as he thought of what was to come, only sadness. He closed his eyes, thinking of Cassie's kiss and the warmth of her body next to his. It had been good. Better than that, really. As they'd moved against each other, he'd been imagining a lifetime of days and nights. The joy in him had been profound, unlike anything he'd felt.

He wished he could have a little more of that life, another afternoon like yesterday, or maybe a wasted week. If not, it was probably just as well things were ending. He did not want to muddle along for decades with people pestering him about getting an heir and assuring the succession. He was not going to marry without love, just to satisfy the Crown.

As Landers walked back to him with a pistol, a

carriage appeared in the distance, the horses racing towards the open field where they stood. Was someone coming to stop them?

He watched it, numb. But as it came closer, his curiosity grew, turning to dread. It stopped near Septon and his second and a cloaked woman leapt out rushing to the two men. He heard a faint, shrill voice arguing against the two calm male voices.

He'd been hoping it was Portia, come to stop her husband from doing something foolish. He was not so lucky. Cassie had found them, just as he'd feared she might.

He sighed, focusing inward and trying to keep his nerves steady. No matter her reason for coming, what he needed to do would be infinitely more difficult now that she was here.

A part of him wanted to go to her, to prostrate himself and beg for absolution. Or one last, perfect kiss before dying. It would be the stuff of poetry and a fitting end. Even in hell, he could survive on that final taste of her lips.

He shook his head and muttered, 'Rot.' Then, he went back to checking the gun Landers had handed him. It did not matter if it was loaded or not, but it was nice to keep busy. When he could find no other reason to delay, he walked forward to meet Julian in the centre of the open ground.

Cassie was waiting there, as well. She stared at him, and he could not look away. 'I read your letter,' she said.

'You were not supposed to see it until breakfast,' he replied.

'Stop this,' she said, holding out a hand to him. 'We need to talk.'

'It is too late for that,' he said, shaking his head. 'What I am doing is for the best.'

'For whom?'

'For you,' he said firmly. 'I think your brother and I agree that you deserve the best future possible. That is not with me.' He reached for her, lifted one of her hands to his lips, then dropped it again and turned to face Julian, who gestured to the side.

'Stand out of the way, Cassandra.'

She turned to him as well, hands on hips. 'I told you yesterday that I am tired of you telling me what to do. I know my own mind. And I am going to marry Sebastian.'

'We agreed a few hours ago that you were not going to marry anyone,' Julian said in the reasonable voice men used with women when they were annoyed. 'And that you were going back to the country to live with the Fisks.'

'Circumstances have changed,' she said. She was not smiling, but his heart leapt.

'I was under the impression that he had not asked for your hand,' Julian said. 'He has not asked me, at least.' He looked past her, glaring at Sebastian. 'If he had, the answer would have been no.'

'We are all aware of your opinion,' Cassie said with a dramatic sigh. 'As I said before, it does not signify.' Then, she threw herself in front of Sebastian, arms spread wide and body pressed intimately into his. 'Now put down the pistols before someone is hurt.'

Julian did not move, but Sebastian whispered into her perfect ear, which was very near to his mouth. 'Let go of me for a minute and I will put it aside.'

He pushed at her with his free hand but she did not budge, following him to the ground as he crouched and set his weapon aside.

'Cassie,' Julian said in a warning voice. 'You need to move.'

She reached behind her, hands fluttering for a moment before locking onto his hips and pulling him tight to her bottom in a way that was uncomfortably intimate for a public setting. 'Julian, if you shoot him, I swear that I shall never speak to you again.'

Sebastian squirmed, trying to put some space between them. But as it had been when they were by the fishpond, her hold was tight and hard to dislodge. 'Cassandra,' he said softly. 'There will be time for this later. But now, you must release me.' He swallowed nervously, fighting the first sparks of desire. 'Let me go or I swear, I shall die.'

'Do not talk of death,' she said, pressing herself even closer to him and nestling her hips into his groin. 'If my brother shoots you, I might not be able to save you this time.'

'This time?' Julian interjected.

'The last time, you were trying to save your brother, not me,' Sebastian reminded her.

'That was last year.' She planted her feet wide and refused to move.

He was painfully aware of each movement, the way their bodies aligned, his manhood shifting to nudge between her legs.

If she noticed, she gave no sign, but said, 'As I told Julian, circumstances have changed.'

'Changed in what way? What do you mean by last year? You had not met until our ball.' Julian's questions were louder, more insistent and not of interest to either of them.

'Changed in what way?' Sebastian whispered urgently.

'Today, I am here to save you. Only you.' Her head lolled back on his shoulder and she grabbed one of his hands, holding it against her waist. 'A year ago, I hardly knew you.' Then she turned her head and whispered so low that only he could hear. 'But I know you, now. I could know you much better, if you let me.'

The words sizzled in his blood, and his head filled with possibilities.

He took a breath and removed his hand from her ribs. 'That is…very flattering, Miss Fisk.' He cleared his throat. 'But, if you continue teasing me in this manner, things will not end well for me.'

'Whyever for?' she said.

Because he was as stiff as the mast of the *Victory*.

He cleared his throat again, trying to think of a way to explain. 'I am indisposed. If you could, perhaps, give me a little space…' But if she did, it would reveal his unfortunate condition to Julian who would shoot him in cold blood for assaulting his sister.

'Cassandra, leave the man alone. We can discuss your future at home, over breakfast.'

She raised her head and gave her brother a foul look. 'We have nothing to discuss.' Then, she leaned back to whisper again. 'He will have to shoot through me. I have no intention of moving.'

She looked back to her brother. 'I would rather die alone than live a single day without him, Julian.'

Her brother handed his gun to his second and

pinched the bridge of his nose, as if rejecting the idea. 'Be reasonable.'

She jerked her head to the side, to the place where her carriage waited. 'There is a post-chaise waiting by the tree. The driver will take us to Gretna.'

'It will take days to get there,' he reminded her.

'If it should rain, and the roads become muddy, it could take even longer. We could be stranded for a whole week.'

Her voice was like the purr of one of the leopards in the menagerie. It reminded him of how the rough tongue of a cat would feel, licking his body.

He groaned. 'Cassandra. What did I just tell you about not teasing me. There are autonomic reactions that are awkward in public.'

'Days and days where I have no hope of rescue,' she said, her lips hot against his ear. 'I shall be all alone. Unchaperoned in the clutches of a scoundrel. Anything could happen to me.'

'Cassie.'

'Lurid acts that I cannot imagine. Debauchery. Depravity. Licentiousness,' she said in a breathy voice. 'I will be helpless to stop you as you fulfill your every wicked fantasy upon my unresisting body.'

Now he gripped her shoulders, holding her in front of him. 'Gods, woman. Show mercy.'

'Westbridge!' Julian was looking around him, probably hoping to retrieve his pistol.

'Julian, go home,' she said with a voice that brooked no nonsense. Then, she turned the same tone on Sebastian. 'Walk with me towards the carriage, and no harm will come to you.'

Keeping her in front of him, he edged to the side, working his way in the direction she indicated.

'Release my sister, you degenerate!' Julian yelled.

'She is the one who has me,' he said, his voice sounded high and nervous as if he was about to laugh or cry.

'I will not let him,' Cassie yelled. 'Not for a lifetime.'

'Cassandra, this is…is…not wise,' Julian said helplessly.

'I have been wise,' she called to him with a laugh. 'But now, more than anything, I want to be happy.'

'Happy?' Sebastian said, shocked to hear the word.

'Happy,' she repeated. 'Now, stay behind me. I don't think he will shoot you if you do so.'

'You don't think?' he said, shocked again. But he did as she suggested and she continued to work her way towards the carriage. When they reached it, he opened the door, hopped inside it and pulled her up after him.

'Drive!' he shouted, as she sprawled in his lap scrabbling for a grip on the upholstery to keep from being bounced off him to the floor.

Then he threw his arms around her, pulling her close so he could kiss her. He was no less comfortable, but the prospect of relief was as near as full daylight.

When they had to stop for breath, he stared at her, amazed. 'You came for me.'

'I would have the first time, as well,' she said. 'If I had known you as I do now.'

'I was not worthy of you,' he said. 'I still am not…'

She put a finger to his lips. 'I refuse to hear another word of such nonsense. You are the only man who showed the slightest interest in what might make me happy.'

He reached to take her hand, pulling it away from his mouth only to bring it back for a kiss. 'You shall have everything you want, if you will only be mine.'

'Then, I do not want to live in London,' she said.

'We must be there for the Season,' he said. 'But the rest of the year will be spent at my home in Leicestershire.'

'I thought you did not like the place,' she said.

'If you are there, it will be paradise,' he replied, kissing her again. 'You shall have a beehive as a wedding gift.'

'Tempting,' she said, smiling. 'And I will allow no more nonsense from you. No foolish self-destruction, no dueling, no scandal.'

'I shall be as boring as your brother is now,' he said, placing her hand on his heart. 'You will even sleep unmolested until we are properly married.'

'Do not take your reformation too far,' she said. 'We are on our way to Scotland. And I meant every word of what I said earlier,' she said, settling more comfortably onto his lap. 'Do as you will with me, you horrible man.'

It was a dream come true. Then, he remembered how he'd expected the day to end and moaned in frustration. 'My darling. My sweet, sweet love. We cannot simply go to Gretna.'

'Hmm?' she said, running a hand down his chest to the buttons on his vest.

'We have no clothes. I did not bring my purse. I was going to my death, this morning. I am totally unprepared.'

'Do you have the ring?' she said, patting his pockets.

'I have carried it everywhere since the day you left me,' he said.

'Then we have everything we need. Thanks to Banks my reticule is full and a hamper had already been packed in the carriage.' She pointed to a wicker basket on the floor. 'He would probably claim it was for my trip home, but there are two glasses for the wine.'

'Good old Banks,' Sebastian said.

'Also bread and cheese. And I believe there are strawberries.'

'I love strawberries,' he said. 'And you, of course.' He sighed and kissed her again. 'I love you. Have done from the first.' He looked past her to the hamper on the floor of the carriage, rummaged around a bit and produced a berry, dangling it in front of her mouth.

She pulled her lips back and tipped her head up so she could grab it with her teeth, sucking for a moment before taking a bite.

He growled. 'For a vicar's daughter, you are surprisingly skilled at seduction.'

'You would know,' she said, narrowing her eyes. 'You have far too much experience on the subject.'

'Only because I wished to be ready when the right woman came along,' he said. 'I wanted to be worthy of her.'

'And am I the right woman?' she said, finishing the berry and licking her lips.

'The one and only,' he assured her.

'Good. Because I might have been infatuated with

you a year ago. But now, I have fallen in love. It does not matter that I know you are wicked. I am yours.'

'All that is over.' He laid his hand on his heart. 'Now that I have you, I will live a life of good works, sobriety and fidelity. And I will give up the lease on the Soho apartment, the minute we return to London.'

She kissed him again, tasting of strawberries, and undid a few more buttons on his waistcoat. 'Oh no, you terrible man. You are keeping the apartment. Or should I say, I am. I expect the keys for a wedding gift. If you promise to be very good… Or perhaps, if you are very, very bad, I will let you visit me there.'

'An interesting proposition,' he said, nuzzling her ear. 'Tell me more.' Then, he reached out to pull the shades on the carriage windows and shut out the world.

Epilogue

December

Though it was still several days until Christmas, the sanctuary of the little church in the village of Septon's Wode had been greened for the season to celebrate the Christening of the Duke's first child. The girl, named Georgiana to honour the duchess's father, was swathed in a gown of linen and lace, her dark hair covered by a cap that had been tatted by her aunt and godmother, the Duchess of Westbridge.

The parents looked on with a mix of pride and nervousness as the vicar held their child over the marble font and murmured the prayers softly so as not to disturb the sleepy babe. Then, he dipped a silver shell into the water below her and poured it over her forehead, which undid his earlier good works.

Georgiana let out a lusty cry and was returned to her mother, who soothed her to silence again.

When the service was over, the vicar led parents and godparents to the church register to see that the details of the baptism were properly recorded.

'Did you ever imagine that a day would come when you would see my name recorded as a potential guardian to your child, Septon?' As he often did, Sebastian was hiding his true feelings behind a joke. But after eight months of marriage, Cassie knew him well enough to understand how touched he'd been that his old friend had given him this honour.

Her brother responded in kind, with a wry smile and a taunt. 'I am surprised enough that you were able to enter a church without turning to dust as you crossed the threshold. But I suppose, since you are married to my sister, I must make some allowances.'

'And to ask you to watch over our little girl,' Portia said, rolling her eyes.

'Your father had a similarly bad idea when he set Julian to watch over you,' Cassie said with a laugh.

'Because men such as us have seen how gentlemen behave when there are no ladies to civilize them,' Sebastian said with a knowing nod. 'We cannot be fooled by scoundrels.'

'Cassandra seems happy enough,' Julian said with a shrug. 'She was most particular when I was trying to find her a husband. If she was willing to settle for you, you cannot be all bad.'

'It is not settling, Julian,' she said with a smile. 'Sebastian has made me a duchess. And he is so desperately grateful to have me that he lets me do whatever I please.'

'Because I know how lucky I am,' her husband said, taking her hand. Then, he smiled at her in a way that was very different from his usual, wicked grin. The look he gave her now was filled with such undisguised love that her eyes filled with tears.

She blinked them away and glanced at the church register, wondering if she had the nerve to ask the question that had weighed on her mind since she'd come to her brother's property. 'Julian,' she said, biting her lip. 'How familiar are you with the records of this parish?'

Her brother laughed. 'I suppose I am listed in them somewhere. I was born at the manor, after all.'

'Is there a chance I might be, as well?'

He looked surprised, as did Portia. Even little Georgiana turned her head as if sensing a change in the room.

She felt Sebastian's hand tighten on her own.

'I don't know,' Julian admitted. 'But we shall look, if you wish.'

She nodded, and the vicar stepped aside so they could page back through the book until they got to the year of Cassie's birth. And there, in a line halfway down the page she saw a record of the christening of Cassandra Perry, the natural born daughter of Margaret Perry, with no father listed.

She stared at the name for a moment, unsure of what she was to do with this information. While she'd never lacked for love in her life, there was room in her heart for more. She looked to the vicar, hoping he might remember the woman listed there.

He shook his head. 'I am sorry to say, Margaret passed not long after you were born. But it is an old family in the village.' He gave her an encouraging smile. 'Your grandfather is a cabinet maker.'

'The Fisks were both alone in the world, the last in their families. It was why they had been so eager to adopt me.' She looked at Sebastian, amazed. 'But now, I have a grandfather.'

'You have other family, as well,' the vicar added. 'Aunts, uncles and many cousins.'

'We must visit them,' Sebastian said.

'We were leaving for your home, this afternoon,' she reminded him. 'We wanted to arrive by Christmas Eve.'

'It is our home,' he reminded her. 'And the Perrys will be my family, just as they are yours. If you wish to meet them, we will take all the time you like.'

'You have to stay for the Christening breakfast, at

the very least,' Portia said. 'We will invite your family to join us, for there is more than enough food.'

Georgiana, wiggled in her arms and let out a hiccupping laugh, raising a balled fist towards her father, who extended a finger for her to grasp.

'We already have so many reasons to celebrate,' Julian said, shaking his daughter's hand.

'We do indeed,' Sebastian agreed. 'I had hoped when the year began that I might find the woman I loved. But I never imagined that we would end it as brothers.' He smiled at Portia. 'Or that I would have such a charming sister. If such wonders can occur in a few months' time, who knows what the new year might bring?' Then, he raised Cassie's hand to his lips and led her out of the church, into the bright winter day.

* * * * *

If you enjoyed this story, be sure to read Christine Merrill's previous instalment in the Wicked Dukes miniseries

To Wed a Devilish Duke

And why not check out her The Irresistible Dukes miniseries

Awakening His Shy Duchess
A Duke for the Penniless Widow

Or one of Christine Merrill's other captivating historical romances

"A Mistletoe Kiss for the Governess" *in* Regency Christmas Weddings

A Scandalous Match for the Marquess

MILLS & BOON®

Coming next month

THE DUKE'S MEDDLESOME MATCHMAKER
Emily E K Murdoch

Book 1 in The Unconventional Oliver Sisters trilogy

'You are not my client,' said the proposal planner slowly.

Henry turned back to Miss Oliver. 'Absolutely not,' he said firmly.

She examined him for a moment, and heat grew in his chest at the attention. Not because it was her, naturally. He would have felt discomforted if it had been anyone.

'Well,' said Miss Oliver finally. 'Well. That changes things.'

'So you'll stay?' Henry said eagerly. He wouldn't be the one to ruin things for Charles. After all, it had been the one thing their father had asked of him, on his deathbed, Henry's years of medical training still not enough to keep the man he loved alive.

Look after your brother, whatever you do.

The proposal planner stepped down from the dog cart—which he had to assume was a good sign.

'My brother is a good man,' Henry snapped, trying to ignore the heat roaring through his body as she stepped closer. 'I want him to be happy.'

'Even if you think I am some sort of charlatan,' Miss Oliver said, halting before him and gazing up at him through long eyelashes.

Henry swallowed. Charlatan? Yes, that was one word for her. It wouldn't be particularly accurate. *Beauty*. That was more accurate. *Temptress*, for it was tempting to lean down and taste—

He stiffly stepped back, half wondering how he'd managed to get himself into such a situation. *Honestly, man. Pull yourself together!*

Miss Oliver was examining him closely. 'It appears most difficult to please you, Mr. Paisley.'

God in His heaven… 'All I am asking is that you fulfil your agreement with my brother,' was all he could manage. 'He is the only family I have left.'

Something flickered in Miss Oliver's gaze. 'I'll stay,' she said shortly, walking around for her trunk.

Henry almost tripped over his own feet to get out and retrieve it for her. It was the least he could do.

'Good,' he said, handing her the heavy thing. *What did she have in there?* 'I'm glad you're staying.'

'I'm not staying for you!' Miss Oliver bristled. 'I—I am already fatigued by avoiding your displeasure.'

They stood there for a heartbeat, glaring at each other, until Miss Oliver snorted, turned around and stamped over to the inn.

Henry watched her go. *Well!* That would be the last time he'd ever be tempted by Miss Oliver!

Continue reading

THE DUKE'S MEDDLESOME MATCHMAKER
Emily E K Murdoch

Available next month
millsandboon.co.uk